Questing for

Überjoy

Book Three of the Post-Lux Trilogy

Konrad Ventana

iUniverse, Inc.
Bloomington

Questing for Überjoy
Book Three of the Post-Lux Trilogy

iUniverse books may be ordered through booksellers or by contacting:

iUniverse
1663 Liberty Drive
Bloomington, IN 47403
www.iuniverse.com
1-800-Authors (1-800-288-4677)

Because of the dynamic nature of the Internet, any web addresses or links contained in this book may have changed since publication and may no longer be valid. The views expressed in this work are solely those of the author and do not necessarily reflect the views of the publisher, and the publisher hereby disclaims any responsibility for them.

Any people depicted in stock imagery provided by Thinkstock are models, and such images are being used for illustrative purposes only.

Certain stock imagery © Thinkstock.

ISBN: 978-1-4620-2952-5 (sc)
ISBN: 978-1-4620-2954-9 (e)
ISBN: 978-1-4620-2953-2 (dj)

Library of Congress Control Number: 2011910228

Printed in the United States of America

iUniverse rev. date: 7/21/2011

Dedication

In memory of Brian and Ian—this work of literary fiction is dedicated to all the unsung heroes in the ongoing battles against the corruption of the human body and oppression of the creative mind; it is dedicated to those who strived before us, and with us, and to the inspired children of generations to come.

Acknowledgments

The author wishes to thank the travel photographer Tom Dempsey at Photoseek.com for kindly providing the digital photographs of Nepal for the cover and chapter frontispieces of this novel.

The story and characters are fictitious, and the timeless drama of the aspiring hero is certainly more mythical than historical. Following the vital messages found in Book One: *A Desperado's Daily Bread* and Book Two: *The Unbearable Sadness of Zilch*, this final lesson of the Post-Lux Trilogy extends its reach beyond literary allegory to the connotations of the evening stars.

Contents

1. The Disappearance of Überjoy

O rion is a special kind of guy. He is a man's man, a ladies' man, the best man. And soon, although he does not yet know it, Orion is about to embark upon his most significant adventure. Orion is an Eagle Scout, which is a title held for life: *"Once an Eagle, always an Eagle,"* as the saying goes. He is, in fact, descended from a long line of Eagle Scouts and, before that, from a long line of hunter-gatherers that goes as far back as anyone can remember. Orion is a man who is no stranger to high drama. In college, he was the captain of the ski team, a fearless downhill racer. It was during those formative years that he articulated his passion for a majestic beauty that moves in exquisite curves, and he developed thighs like tree trunks. In the summertime, he'd worked as a lifeguard at the local country club, where he was always prepared, although there was never much call, for deep-water rescues.

Orion is a different kind of guy—he is a nice guy who is used to finishing first. Yet he'd give you the shirt off his back if such an occasion would arise, and this must have been fairly common for him, since he always seemed to be wearing more than one shirt at a time in an outdoorsy sort of layered look. Let's just say that he was prepared to give you the shirt off his back and leave it at that. However, something needs to be said from the outset about Orion's habit of finishing first. It was almost as if nature had endowed him with such outstanding athletic prowess as to enable him to dash effortlessly across the most forbidding and inscrutable of landscapes as though he were gaining sustenance directly from the sun, driven not by a hunger for some inimitable victory but by a tireless desire to chase, to pursue, to attain something valuable, regardless of the effort required. By the ripe old age of thirty-five, Orion had attained an inspiring constellation of sought-after accomplishments in the various spheres of his life.

Orion's renowned athletic prowess and success as an iconic sporting entrepreneur was equaled only by his impressive good looks, which offered him an expansive choice of leading ladies. A shock of naturally wavy, dark chocolate hair stood playfully on end when he rubbed his hand through it in either exasperation or consternation. His piercing blue eyes made people wonder if he wore colored contact lenses. His plump, perpetually wet-looking lips peered out behind soft, light brown whiskers, which his fiancée found both endearing and scratchy; he bit his bottom lip whenever he was listening carefully or pondering his next move.

At the point in time in which our story begins, Orion is engaged to be married to the most beautiful woman he has ever seen. A finalist in the Miss Teen Idaho beauty pageant a few years back, the lovely Joycelyn Eberhard is still capable of stopping traffic all the way from Bonners Ferry to the main campus of the University of Idaho, where she recently graduated with a Master of Arts degree in education. The university's College of Letters, Arts & Social Sciences is apparently where Joycelyn adopted the notion that "World Peace" ought to be somewhat more than a convenient rhetorical device used to evoke an emotional response in the audience of a local, or even national, beauty pageant. That is, perhaps, why she was so keen on "doing something earnest and consequential" before settling down and raising a nuclear family, as was generally expected of a young American woman of such obvious natural beauty.

It was the idealistic allure of the Peace Corps that drew Joycelyn Eberhard away from her conventionally anticipated life course, in a personal and somewhat quixotic attempt to do something earnest and consequential in the name of World Peace. Neither Orion nor any of

Joycelyn's closest friends or family members—all of whom fondly referred to the quondam beauty queen as their own *Überjoy*—could fully comprehend her unnecessarily idealistic motivations. They could no more comprehend her decision to join the Peace Corps as a volunteer teacher than they could hide their dismay at the very thought that their Überjoy would forsake her dashing fiancé, her friends, and her family for the starkness of a cold, two-room schoolhouse on the other side of the planet. It bears mentioning that this particular two-room schoolhouse is located in the Khumjung Sherpa village, high in the Himalayan Mountains of Nepal.

Although it galled Orion, this strident man of action, to wait upon anything or anyone, let alone something as near and dear to him as the woman he intended to marry, Orion knew that Joycelyn Eberhard was a woman worth waiting for. And so, there was nothing he could do but tarry through the long winter and the spring and the summer until the coming of the fall, when his beautiful, starry-eyed fiancée was scheduled to return from her idealistic sojourn to Nepal—nothing he could do but wait with uncharacteristic forbearance for his Überjoy to return.

Amid the autumn of his discontent—it was September, and Überjoy was to return in late November—Orion trained with the Sun Valley Ski Patrol, striving to keep in top shape for the upcoming ski season. Orion was striding briskly along as the pale, yawning arms of the morning mists rose up as if in surrender to a greater glory ascending in the brightening blue sky. The last crystalline vestiges of nature's dewy tears were silently sublimating from the forest paths as the enduring soles of a dozen high-tech running shoes appeared and pummeled the ground. There was a rasping sound of chainsaws coming from the direction of Dollar Mountain, and the sweet, greasy smells of damp leaves and wood smoke hung redolent in the air. Orion was striding briskly along the Wood River trails, freshly garnished with newly fallen leaves that would soon be blown away or covered with snow in the coming months. As usual, he was racing far out in front of his fellow ski patrollers, who were casually chatting and joking while jogging comfortably along with the uniformly measured cadence of their pleasant, postmodern lives. Following the old Union Pacific Railroad route through the Wood River Valley, the rustic trail looped around Elkhorn Village and eventually connected with a paved roadway that ran on into Sun Valley proper. Yes, it is in the autumn of Orion's discontent when we first observe him striding briskly along; and then he is briskly striding past, leaving the poetic chiasmus of this introductory moment far behind.

When Orion arrived back at the resort complex, he was alarmed to find Joycelyn's father and the Blaine County sheriff standing at the entrance of the circular driveway in front of the main lodge to meet him.

"This can't be good news," said Orion, still breathing hard from the running.

"No, son, it's not good at all," said Joycelyn's father, shaking his head. "It appears that she's been taken from us!"

"What do you mean, *taken?*" asked Orion. "Who took her where?"

Orion studied the traces of unbearable sadness that strained the ruggedly handsome visage of Joycelyn's father, who slowly averted his eyes, and then he studied the weather-beaten face of the grizzled old Western sheriff for additional clues. Orion squinted hard into the leaden eyes of the seasoned lawman, who appeared to have seen too much trouble, too much inhumanity, too much criminal activity, and too much pitiable human drama to be either surprised or alarmed by anything under this old sun. There was nothing there to behold but gray and gloom and more lead.

"Who took her where?" repeated Orion.

Suddenly overcome by the grief he had obviously been trying hard to control, Joycelyn's father started sobbing in low, mournful tones. Orion and the Blaine County sheriff helped the weeping man into a cedar lawn chair, and Orion planted a consoling hand upon his shoulder.

"We don't have answers to those questions yet," said the sheriff.

"But you *do* know that Joycelyn is still alive? You *can* tell me that much, at least?"

"I'm afraid not," said the sheriff. "China is a mighty long way from here."

"China!!!" shouted Orion. He was beside himself for a brief moment, struggling with the weight of catastrophe while striving to be of some comfort to the stricken father of his would-be fiancée. He stifled his indignant outburst enough to mutter a rhetorical question. "How in the world did my beloved Überjoy get taken to China?"

By now, Orion's fellow ski patrollers had arrived on the scene, breathless and panting, and there was clearly more heat than light to be thrown onto the subject. Eventually it would be discerned that very little information was available at this time—other than the news that Joycelyn and several other teachers were missing from the Khumjung Village school, along with a number of female students, and that there were numerous reports of Maoist rebel activities in the area. Other than that, the Peace Corps officials apparently had no additional information.

Not a man to stand around wringing his hands for long, Orion pointed out that they needed to get some real answers *tout de suite*. After regaining his composure, Orion's forthcoming father-in-law said that he was feeling well enough to make some calls to the State Department and the Foreign Services.

Orion nodded and bit his bottom lip, recalling that the man had several business associates in, shall we say, high places. Orion thought for a moment or two longer, and then he asked, "Where can I find the regional headquarters of the Peace Corps?"

Joycelyn's father looked up, and their eyes met as he replied, "Seattle."

Along the promenades of Seattle's Westlake Center, horses bearing uniformed policemen trotted, musicians strummed acoustic guitars, and brass horns blared. Hordes of busy people came and went on buses, streetcars, and monorails, dining under festive outdoor canopies and shopping in the fashion malls. The numberless granite face of a pedestal clock was wrapped in the embrace of a large, stainless-steel question mark that forever raised the most haunting question—*for whom does this silent face now toll?* No one seemed to be the slightest bit aware of the great disaster that had befallen them. No one even seemed to notice that Überjoy had been taken away.

"I'm sorry, but there is nothing we can do but wait for more intelligence," said the Regional Director of the Peace Corps, a nondescript little man in a pinstripe suit behind a large mahogany desk. "The Chief of Operations is in direct contact with the Director of International Volunteerism who is in direct contact with the Director of Asia Operations who is in direct contact with the Director of Crisis Management who is in direct contact with the Director of Communications. It's really the best that we can do, under the circumstances. You know, our hands are tied when it comes to such matters," he said as he interlaced his fingers complacently and hunched his narrow shoulders. "All I can tell you is that the safety and welfare of our Peace Corps volunteers is always among our top priorities."

"There must be someone I can speak with to get some actual information concerning Joycelyn's mission and her itinerary," said Orion, leaning heavily on his hands, which were now planted firmly on the polished surface of the executive's desk. "After all, someone had to swear her into this Gipsy circus."

"That particular kind of information would be made available to the Director of Volunteer Recruitment and Selection, or possibly the Associate Director of Volunteer Support, but those offices are located in Washington, DC," he quipped, completely unfazed by Orion's intimidating display.

"Come now. You can do better than that. This is the US government, for pity sake." Orion pushed himself hard off of the polished mahogany surface and began pacing in front of the oversized desk. "Suppose that *your* fiancée went off to god knows where to teach some third-world children a thing or two, and then you suddenly found out that she was missing and unaccounted for and that no one could tell you where she is, who she was taken by, or even whether she is dead or alive." Orion stopped abruptly and pressed his weight onto the mahogany desk again. "Can you really expect me to stand calmly by and wait until your departmental directorial daisy chain finishes communicating with … with itself?"

"There is no need to get rude with me. There is no joy in this for me either. I expect that I would feel exactly the same as you, if I were in your position. But as an officer of the Peace Corps, I have to accept the fact that I occupy a position of great bureaucracy in an increasingly unstable world, and accepting that fact, I have to work for increased stability through international directorates that lead, through education and example, to a renewed appreciation of the virtues of our great bureaucracy."

Orion realized that he was getting nowhere. He was obviously confronting the very same kind of purposeless mentality that would have the entire population walking for the cure, running for the cure, treading water, and spinning its proverbial wheels for the cure—a cure that would finance the construction of many lofty edifices and officious institutions—but without the involvement of real-life heroes, it would be an elusive cure that would never come. Orion concluded that this Regional Director's notion of World Peace, as a placid acceptance of some global bureaucratic unanimity, was a peace that would come at too great a price for him to even consider, let alone accept. He would seek his Überjoy, he would find his Überjoy, and, come hell or high water, he would have his beloved Überjoy back in his muscular arms again.

Orion began to pace the floor like a caged snow leopard. "Please, in the name of all that is sacred and holy and endangered, tell me who I can speak with to get some *useful* intelligence to formulate a *useful* plan of action."

"Oh, that's easy. That would be the Director of Field Assistance and Applied Research. I'll see if she's in …" he added as he pressed a button on the oversized telephone stationed on his mahogany desk and listened carefully for an assuring ring.

Orion was soon ushered into the office of a comely, middle-aged woman in tasteful business attire who rose from her chair behind a duplicate executive desk, introduced herself as Miss Helena Hypatia and asked him if he would care for some tea. Orion found himself staring awkwardly at the graceful yet determined movements of this urbane Director of Field Assistance and Applied Research as she prepared the ceremonial teapot. Then, catching himself in the foible, he quickly apologized by admitting that she just happened to remind him of a splendid teacher of mathematics he had known a long, long time ago. "I don't mean to offend you by my gauche historical reference, but this particular math teacher was a fine woman that I truly admired."

"Oh, I'm not offended in the least," she said, pouring out the tea with consummate precision. "I myself was a teacher of mathematics and natural sciences, that is, before I became an administrator." She sipped her tea and leaned forward on her desk, steepling her fingers and fixing Orion with a keen and practiced stare. "I consider the cultivation of the mind and the profession of teaching to be a great honor, as well as a great responsibility. For fifteen years," she said as she smiled, emphasizing the duration without giving Orion the space to so much as clear his throat of exasperation, "I worked in inner-city schools and challenged communities with high immigrant populations, which only served to increase my appreciation of the need for cross-cultural education. The Peace Corps provided me with the opportunity to expand my commitment and involvement to an international level. Not only do our volunteers disseminate practical knowledge, provide leadership, and spread goodwill to underdeveloped nations around the world, but they bring a better understanding and appreciation of cultural diversity back home with them, when they return to our society and our classrooms in the States."

Orion had slowly sipped his tea with as much patience and politeness as he could muster throughout her sales pitch; now he pounced on her moment of pause and blurted out his single-minded purpose: "I'm happy for you. Really I am. But one of your blasted international Peace-Love programs has run amuck. One of your well-intended teachers, one who just happens to be my fiancée, has fallen off the face of the earth, and nobody around here seems to know or even care what happened to her." Orion's eyes sparkled with intensity as he spoke. "You want to cultivate some great responsibility? How about beginning by helping me to find out exactly what happened to Joycelyn Eberhard ... and then you can tell me exactly what you intend to do right now to get her safely back into a US classroom." Orion could be quite formidable when he rose to his full stature, as he did now in extreme earnest.

"Oh, is that why you're here? I did hear something about that awful business in Nepal. It is most unfortunate," said the urbane director as she placed her teacup back in its saucer on the large executive desk and looked vaguely out the window. "Is that why you're here?" she asked again, obviously confused and somewhat embarrassed by the recruitment speech that she was accustomed to offering up, on any and all occasions.

"Why else?" snapped Orion. "What could be more important than the news that an American Peace Corps worker, one of the most beautiful girls in all of America, mind you, has been taken off the reservation ... most likely kidnapped ... right out from under your noses?" Orion, the caged snow leopard, began to pace again. "What could possibly be more important than protecting the safety and welfare of an American citizen on official government business? And if you tell me *world peace*, I swear I'm going to puke this high tea all over your mahogany desk."

The director frowned, and a hint of concern crossed her face. "But you must know that our hands are tied when it comes to such matters?"

"Yeah, I know." Orion stopped pacing and faced her. "I heard that from the other guy down the hall. Look here, Miss Helena Hypatia, you tell me that you were once a school teacher—that is, before you became an administrator, or a recruiter, or a cheerleader, or whatever you are. Isn't there anything you can tell me that I couldn't get off the side of a box of breakfast cereal?"

Helena Hypatia appeared to be considering the virtue of truth over dogma.

"Please, ma'am, I'm desperate and I don't know where else to turn.

She has been gone for almost a year now, and we were scheduled to be married when she gets back home to Idaho in about two months." Orion's head was bowed by the weight of his grief.

Slowly, the mysterious wheels of the cosmos began to turn in a rational direction, and the Director of Field Assistance and Applied Research turned her refined mind from the political *esprit de corps* to the astronomical problem at hand. "You say that Joycelyn was scheduled to return to the US in two months?" queried Hypatia.

"Yes, ma'am," said Orion, rubbing his hand through his hair and resting it for a moment on the soft ends now standing straight up. "She was supposed to be back home by the end of November."

"That's quite curious," Hypatia said as she poured herself and Orion the bitter dregs. "Something just doesn't add up," she added, waxing downright mathematical. "First of all, I am surprised to hear you speak of Miss Eberhard as your fiancée. You see, being in a serious relationship is a red flag that could have prevented her from being accepted into the Peace Corps volunteer program in the first place. And secondly, there is a discrepancy between the one year of service that you have apparently been led to believe, and the actual span of more than two years, which is the standard term for a Peace Corps volunteer—three months of training, plus the standard two-year assignment. Can you explain this disparity in chronological time to me?"

"No, I most certainly cannot. And I'm not sure I like what you're getting at."

Orion suddenly stopped pacing and sunk back into the chair, a snow leopard not only caged by tragic circumstance but blindsided by an unanticipated shot to the heart.

Miss Helena Hypatia must have felt a certain amount of sympathy for both Orion and his joyous, if not entirely honest, fiancée. After all, she must have known the sacrifices that a woman must make to gain her own personal freedom of *choice* and of *thoughtfulness*, and to serve a thankless society in the noble robes of an educator. She began to brief Orion about the social and political situation in Nepal, stopping short of revealing any incriminating details about direct US involvement.

"Nepal, like Tibet before it, is caught in the grips of an ongoing struggle between the aggressive expansionism of Communist China and the fragile ideals of democracy that are, unfortunately, foisted under the auspices of a corruptible and wholly ineffectual monarchy. The result has been the emergence of yet another insidious, undeclared war, as we have seen on other occasions, from Korea to Vietnam. That being said, the so-called 'People's War' of the Nepalese Maoists is, in actuality, mortal combat conducted in slow motion, both geographically and politically. In this protracted yet undeclared war, the Maoist insurgency has been fighting against the Royal Nepalese Army and other unnamed supporters of the doomed monarchy."

"Is this the same monarchy that was nearly wiped out by some kind of massacre in the royal palace?" asked Orion as he rose from his chair and began pacing again. "I heard about those killings when Joycelyn was first considering her assignment. She told me that everything was all right now, and that a new and better prince or king was in control. Or was she lying about that too?"

"Well, not exactly," she said patiently, following his movements. "It's true that a new king is in control of the government, but only tenuously. It appears that the intrigue and the suspicions surrounding the massacre of the royal family, compounded by certain ill-advised attempts to quell the insurgency by brutal police action and military force, have only served to strengthen the resolve of the revolutionaries, who continue to gain support while the political situation is rapidly deteriorating from within."

Orion paused at the window, the gravity of the situation she'd described washing over him. Without turning his head, he asked the question he already knew the answer to: "You mean to tell me that you sent unarmed American men and women into a war zone?" He turned, but she refused to meet his gaze. "You mean to tell me," he continued, his voice barely above a whisper now, his pain and disappointment unabashedly apparent, "that you sent a beautiful, talented, idealistic

American woman to the front lines of an undeclared war, like a sheep in the midst of wolves?"

Hypatia paused. She closed her eyes and cleared her throat. "Honestly, yes," she said, her voice soft and clear. "That is what we do." She replaced her teacup in its saucer. "We try and fight the insidious cancer from the inside. We strive to set an example of the virtues of education, ingenuity, practicality, scientific innovation, and democracy *vis-à-vis* the inner darkness of oppression, coercion, brutality, and the blatant tyranny fomented by the uneducated, often fanatical, masses."

"You intentionally sent my Überjoy as a sheep among the wolves, even though you knew that the situation was dicey and deteriorating, and that there was nothing but risk, and more risk, to her safety." Orion slowly shook his head with an obvious expression of disdain. "There ought to be a law against such irresponsible behavior."

"Assuredly, if the political situation were to worsen substantially, I am certain that our volunteers would have been recalled and evacuated. But you must understand that Joycelyn was not uninformed of the risks. As a volunteer teacher, she was well aware of the challenges of implementing her own heartfelt American idealism in the context of political uncertainty. She, and many others like her, chose to serve at the forefront of a greater war: that is, a war against ignorance, superstition, religious and even political fanaticism that would propel the world into a new dark age, an age of the *inner dark.*"

"I think I understand your motivations, and perhaps even hers," Orion said with a raised eyebrow followed by an angry chomp upon his lower lip. "But really, isn't it a bit dubious sending volunteers into unstable political situations, considering that the undeclared war in Nepal is getting worse and our side doesn't appear to be winning?"

"On the contrary, there are many of us who truly believe that the pernicious aspects of despotic communism and revolutionary Maoism, and many other forms of virulent extremism, are doomed to extinction with the judicious application of high-minded Western values, proper education, modernization, and general goodwill, tinctured with a resulting rise of affluence."

"Okay, supposing I agree with you. Supposing I even share your sense of purpose to some extent. What can I do right now ... what can *we* do right now ... to rescue Joycelyn from the Maoists?" Orion paused, and he prodded the scattered remnants of soggy tea leaves arrayed in the bottom of his cup as if he were attempting to rearrange the Fates themselves with the tip of his index finger. "Or will that require more tea?"

Miss Helena Hypatia simply smiled at Orion and, considering his question to be a formal request, prepared another pot of steaming hot water. And then she dropped a hypothetical bombshell. "The reason that I took the time to outline the political situation in Nepal for you is that I don't think that the Maoists pose the greatest danger to Joycelyn ... and never did."

"Really, do tell."

"I'm going to go out on a limb here, philosophically speaking ... and before I do, I need to know that you understand, as I understand, the limits of the reliability and the repeatability of what I am about to tell you—about the true forces of darkness that may be at work here."

"Yes, ma'am ... definitely. That's why I'm here. As a decisive man of action, I need to know what you know—what you *really* know. I mean, what you understandably cannot say with any certainty—at risk of being wrong or politically incorrect—but can tentatively conclude with a reasonable degree of freedom, based on your applied research in the field. Please tell me about the true forces of darkness that may be involved in the disappearance of my beloved Überjoy."

The tea was served piping hot this time, hot enough to scald the uninitiated, but not enough to dissuade a true connoisseur who savors the flavor of actuality cast amongst the misty verisimilitudes of the steaming vapors.

"I fear that Joycelyn Eberhard, your Überjoy, as you call her, may have fallen prey to a monstrous evil that has emerged unheralded, not only in Nepal, but in the entire region. That is, the problem of human trafficking—particularly of girls and young women—to indentured servitude and brothels in India and elsewhere. Each year, from five thousand to seven thousand girls and women are trafficked from Nepal to India alone for the commercial sex trade. Due to the clandestine nature of the crime, accurate figures are difficult to extract, but the problem appears to be increasing every year with the deteriorating security and economic conditions and the general atmosphere of lawlessness that prevails."

Orion opened his mouth, but nothing came out. He sunk into his chair and, for a moment, he wasn't sure that he had heard the Director of Field Assistance and Applied Research correctly. Perhaps in his devastation over the idea of his woman missing, he'd begun to hallucinate. Human trafficking? Commercial sex trade? These concepts did not mix at all well with his own conceptions of Überjoy.

But Miss Helena Hypatia continued to expand upon her suspicions. Testing the steaming tea with adroit sips, she continued, "The forces of darkness I am referring to are the deadly demons of superstition, illiteracy, gender disparity, cultural stereotypes, caste systems, and economic deprivation, all of which place women in peril … it places them in nonnegotiable situations that they are completely powerless to either avoid or resist. And I can assure you that these forces of darkness are far more treacherous, far more intransigent, and far more malignant than the lure of Stalinism, Marxism, or even Chinese Communism when all is said and done."

"You're talking about the wholesale trafficking of women and children, in this day and age? You've got to be kidding," Orion said as his eyes widened with surprise. "This is the twenty-first century, for goodness sake. Sex slaves marched across international borders in broad daylight? You can't be serious!"

But Miss Helena Hypatia was neither kidding nor smiling nor even blinking as she returned his look, which sent a violent chill down Orion's spine. He took a big gulp of the scalding hot tea and a deep breath before he continued his inquiry.

"You're talking about slavery … real *Heart of Darkness* stuff … and you're serious?" asked Orion, hoping against hope that she was not.

"Deadly serious," was all she said, with a finality that nearly crushed the life's blood from Orion's deeply wounded but still frantically beating heart.

"And you have good reason to believe that Joycelyn and the schoolchildren she was caring for have been taken prisoner by such scoundrels?"

"Now you know what you need to know ... what I in good conscience, but not in my official capacity, was able to tell you. The only question remaining is whether or not you will be able to put this valuable information to good use in an urgent plan of action before it is too late." The latter clause of this rhetorical interrogatory was equally chilling.

"I want to thank you sincerely for telling me the truth of the matter as you see it," said Orion as he rose slowly from the chair. "In my mind, that makes you a woman of epic virtue. Still, I wish that you could give me more information on how best to proceed from here."

"I can only tell you that *time is always of the essence*, nothing more."

If the sound of a tree falling in the forest of the human soul makes a sound, then the world at large might have been awakened from its slumber. As it were, Orion, the hunter-gatherer-Eagle Scout absorbed the information with the stoic resolve of a true hero and politely bid farewell to the magnanimous Peace Corps director. As he made his heavyhearted way to the outer chamber of the director's office, Miss Helena Hypatia escorted him to the doorway. And then, quite curiously, she asked Orion where he would be staying while he was gathering information in Seattle. She smiled when he told her he was checked in at the Mayflower. They shook hands in an extended affiliation, and her handshake was firm and warm and somewhat reassuring. Then she covered his firmly clasped hand with her other hand and offered Orion a final note of philosophical advice.

"When circumstances seem to be insurmountable, and you find yourself at the end of your rope, please remember that optimism can often be more useful than despair."

Orion walked out onto the Westlake promenade in the general direction of the major department stores of an upscale shopping center—he was a man lost in the chaos of his own immediate surroundings, a man struggling to make sense of a modern world that appeared to him to have lost all sense of perspective, if not common decency. Stepping sideways to avoid bumping shoulders with a group of giggling girls laden with shopping bags, Orion paused briefly to watch a woman and a young girl—presumably mother and daughter, both expensively dressed—entering a designer boutique. The pair was flushed with the rush of conspicuous consumerism and utterly oblivious. The crestfallen man raised his collar against a creeping chill and moved toward the hollow glamour of more trendy boutiques, resisting the urge to stop shoppers and plead with them to open their eyes—to see the menacing glare of the harsh realities that continued to exist in this world. Could they not hear the distant screams of its latest victims? Were they not aware that women and children continued to remain at risk, and if we did not act in time, that all may soon be lost? Would no one other than he—who long ago dedicated his life to saving people and hunting things that were lost or in distress—join in this impossible, outlandish, unreasonable quest that had been so suddenly and so cruelly thrust upon him?

Orion strode quickly past a bearded man with a cardboard sign who was preaching plaintively to passersby. Alas, the once-treasured story of the savior at the Garden of Gethsemane now seemed to Orion like a childhood fairy tale as he personally and unavoidably confronted the monstrous maw of an inauspicious nature that led one from the dusk of disillusionment to the brink of the *inner dark*.

Orion deeply appreciated the new information he had gained, no matter how grim, and yet in gaining this knowledge, he also realized that he was no longer innocent. He was no longer blind to the desperate needs and the pathos of the uncivilized world at large. In his rude awakening, Orion was forced to realize that there were still real monsters and dragons that had yet to be hunted down and slain.

Moreover, he was forced to realize that these lingering monsters, these internecine demons, were not external to the human condition and could no more be removed with the flight of an arrow or the stroke of a sword than the demons of envy, greed, lust, and predatory behavior could be banished from the human personality; no more than the monstrous ego itself could be removed from the labyrinth of the human psyche.

He knew that, without Joycelyn Eberhard, his previous life as a Boy Scout, lifeguard, downhill racer, ski patroller, and athletic entrepreneur was woefully incomplete, and yet these particular activities had prepared him well for the arduous journey he was about to undertake. As he began to question the value of all his previous values, he started to realize that he may be the only human being alive who was so unreasonably equipped and compelled—compelled by an inexplicable burden of passion and desire, fused with his rather extreme determination and capability—to make such a momentous and irrational decision. For Orion, the decision *not to try* and save his beloved Überjoy would be a far greater tragedy.

Nevertheless, it took heroic effort for Orion to tighten his proverbial belt, to roll up his figurative sleeves, and to choose to try, against all reasonable expectations of success, driven by a dire urgency to pursue this thing regardless, with an unassailable knowledge that his pursuit was for something vital, valuable, beautiful, and human—all too human.

"Spare change?"

Orion looked up, finding it difficult to focus on the man holding out his hand with a strange mixture of hope and resolve that there was no reason for hope. Orion dug into his pocket distractedly and dumped whatever change he could find into the man's hand. Walking on, he asked himself, *Why did Joycelyn feel it necessary to misrepresent the duration of her Peace Corps mission? And why did she fail to reveal their wedding plans to her sponsors?* Perhaps that was the even more troubling question.

He tried to shake these questions from his mind in a hurry. And as he advanced, a larger-than-life poster in black and white flashed by showing a girl, not as beautiful as Joycelyn, but pretty and pursing her lips seductively. *People lie,* he told himself. *Stories are told every day. Every life is but a fiction from a particular point of view. Even the many scholarly renderings of the lives of ancient heroes, prophets, and saints are really little more than tall tales that are summarily aggrandized by well-meaning people acting with the most enlightened of intentions.* Orion simply loved Joycelyn Eberhard too much to suspect her motives; he knew her too well to conclude that she had been intentionally deceitful; he missed her too much to think of anything but their impassioned reunion—a reunion filled with romance and eroticism and consummate attainment, a reunion filled with endless exultation and exceedingly great joy.

Orion walked stridently, almost unconsciously, from mall to mall and back onto the city streets, lost in the vastness of space between the thoughts, the man, and the evening stars. He was determined, yes. He was resigned, yes. He was in love, yes indeed. But he had absolutely no clue about how to proceed from here—and that was the most depressing thought of all. So depressing was this realization that Orion's broad shoulders began to droop perceptibly, and his once-impressive stride gradually slowed to the ponderous cadence of a funeral dirge. It was nearly evening when Orion finally made his woe-begotten way back to the stately Mayflower Park Hotel, where he would stay the night.

When he approached the main entrance of the hotel, Orion noticed a mysterious man, wearing a gray snap-brim fedora and a telltale trench coat, leaning casually up against the ornate facade of the building while pretending to read the evening newspaper. It was all so ghastly neo-noir, considering the darker shade of realism embodied by Orion's present circumstances, the deepening shadows of his sorrow, the dark corners of the night that were closing in around him, and the general mood of pessimism, alienation, and despair he was feeling at the time. Orion found himself speaking out loud to the mysterious man behind the evening newspaper.

"Brother, don't I wish that men like Sam Spade, Mike Hammer, and Philip Marlowe were still around to help me find my way out of this nightmare."

The mysterious man lowered the evening news, skillfully folded the newspaper into a compact rectangular shape, and tapped it against the palm of his left hand before tucking it away within a deep pocket of his trench coat. An unattended cigarette dangled from the corner of his mouth, supported by a chin that was only slightly less angular than that of Dick Tracy's. His eyes, cynical and gray, weighed and measured Orion, the man, without emotion. "You look like you could use a friend," was all he said.

"And might you be such a friend?" asked Orion, too far gone into the twilight of his own dark corner of the universe to hold anything back.

"That I might," said the man as he dropped the cigarette to the ground and crushed it out with his shoe. "That is, if you are the hunter." Then he turned abruptly with the flourish of a stage magician and began to walk away, down the darkening city street.

Orion followed the mysterious man with the telltale trench coat down Olive Way, along the 5th Avenue flank of the Westlake Center, and onto Pine Street, keeping a respectable distance yet without losing sight of the conspicuous snap-brim fedora. He followed the mysterious man to the Westlake station, where they boarded the monorail heading north to the Seattle Center. The irony of this cozy postmodern mode of transportation was not lost on Orion, who was constantly reminded of the frivolousness and the comfort of his own sheltered world versus the bone-chilling fate of his lovely Peace Corps idealist, an idealist who was obviously left out in the cold.

Upon arriving at the Seattle Center, the mysterious man signaled to Orion with a touch of two fingers to the brim of his fedora. They detrained and proceeded to converge on the entrance of the Space Needle, at which point the man suddenly turned to face Orion and handed him a ticket that read, "Admit One."

"Don't bother asking me anything, hunter. I'm just the tour guide. You know that no one would blame you if you just walked away—but I know that you won't. I can tell that much from the look of you." The man's perceptive eyes gleamed from the penumbra of his downturned hat brim. "There's a party waiting to be crashed up at the SkyCity Restaurant—but remember, where you're going, there won't be any more Philip Marlowe characters around to hold your hand." With that, a cigarette was lit, an angular jaw was clenched, a cynical gray eye was winked, and the man in the gray snap-brim fedora and telltale trench coat disappeared into the crowd.

Orion watched the spot where his guide had disappeared, feeling an unspoken "What?" form on his lips. But his natural instincts guided him onward, and the "Admit One" ticket guided him upward to the revolving disk at the top of the futuristic skyscraper. Rotating on its axis every forty-seven minutes, the swanky restaurant was jam-packed with dinner guests who were busy gazing out at the breathtaking panoramas while basking on genteel renditions of Pacific Northwest cuisine. The leisurely 360-degree rotation of the dining room floor was perceptible but not unnerving to Orion, for it paled in comparison to the dizzying whirl of his ordinary world that was now spiraling out of control.

With the presentation of his ticket, Orion was ushered to a table for one, which seemed curious to him, considering the circumstances. The views of the Olympic Mountains across Puget Sound—enhanced by the restaurant's revolving deck—offered little consolation to the sad heart of the lonely hunter, for the world, as he once knew it, seemed to be all but lost beyond the horizon. Orion ordered the wild salmon without much enthusiasm, and he was struggling to hold onto that one last shred of optimism, as Miss Helena Hypatia had recommended, when he noticed a coaster passing by his advancing table on the stationary sill of the large, angular, plate-glass window—a coaster upon which the words *"Orion rises at sunset"* were handwritten in ink.

Orion grabbed the coaster and looked around the room for someone, anyone, who appeared out of the ordinary. He scanned the tables near the windows, looking for the source of the message, but no one seemed even remotely interested in his curious predicament. His dinner was promptly served without the slightest innuendo of intrigue, with the exceptions that the artisan goat cheese in his arugula salad seemed a bit flakey, and the Chanterelle mushroom ragout was a bit off.

The room and the faces within it grew progressively darker and more obscure with the pending nightfall, when the lights of the Seattle skyline began blinking on like a thousand stars in a deepening, darkening sky. Orion passed on dessert and opted, instead, for Starbucks coffee, wondering how long he would have to wait for something eventful to happen. At about that time, he noticed a dessert menu on the windowsill, passing by his revolving platform. It was barely noticeable at first, lying there obliquely on the shadowy ledge, and he nearly had to lurch out of his seat to retrieve it before it passed beyond his reach.

Inside the dessert menu was a second handwritten note:

Orion Seeking the Lost Pleiad,

Ask, and it will be given to you; seek, and you will find. Prepare yourself for a journey in the wilderness, yet consider the lilies of the field. Do not worry about tomorrow, for tomorrow will have worries of its own. Seek first the kingdom, but do not cast your pearls before swine. When you do a charitable deed, do not sound a trumpet. Enter by the narrow gate. Leave immediately, without hesitation. Look into Helicopter Trekking with Fishtail Air Ltd., Kathmandu.

Regards,
Seven Sisters and Company

After spending the next morning in Seattle, outfitting himself at a local REI store, Orion was on his way to Kathmandu with precious little to go on, but with as much blind love and optimism as he could possibly carry.

2.   A Hero's Journey to Nepal

In addition to blind love and optimism, Orion carried his far-reaching plans for a better future; he carried his personal dream of radiant beauty; he carried the unassailable certainty that he could attain anything and everything he desired with the forceful application of his indomitable will. One might say that he carried the hopes and ambitions of the entire Western world upon his shoulders. A preliminary shuttle bus ride from downtown Seattle to the Vancouver International Airport, and he was soon checking in his newly purchased Gregory Baltoro expedition pack loaded with fifty-plus pounds of the bare essentials of wilderness backpacking—bordering on mountaineering—and an overstuffed REI duffle bag filled with additional dehydrated foodstuffs and a minimalist array of "trad" climbing gear.

He settled into the reclining cubicle of his pod-like business-class compartment, which extended diagonally from the passenger window to the aisle, unlaced his waterproof hiking boots, and breathed a series of anxious sighs. As the 747 jumbo jet taxied onto the runway and roared off into the night, Orion made a mental checklist of all the tangible things he carried into the oblivious sky. He carried basic survival gear for high-altitude trekking conditions, including an oversized windproof expedition parka and windproof pants, weighing 2.9 pounds, a compressible down vest (1.2 pounds), and a midweight fleece jacket (1.4 pounds), in addition to a handpicked selection of high-tech hiking socks, gloves, headgear, shirts, shorts, pants, gaiters, and long underwear. He carried a goose-down, mummy-style "below freezing" sleeping bag, which weighed approximately 5 pounds, complete with its lightweight fleece bag liner and nylon stuff sack. In addition, he had packed a closed-cell foam sleeping pad that weighed another 1.6 pounds. It was with a certain degree of expectation and devotion that he had selected a two-person, tension-truss geodesic tent with its rainfly and groundcover, which together weighed in at nearly 4.8 pounds, rather than the ultralight solo design that weighed only 2.7 pounds. Chalk one up for optimism.

Orion carried the basic "ten essentials" of GMP, or good mountaineering practice, and then some. That is, in addition to the store-bought teahouse trekking maps of Nepal, he carried a 3-ounce Silva Ranger precise azimuth compass with adjustable declination and foldout mirror for accurate sightings. He carried a waterproof xenon headlamp with rotating focus bezel (6.5 ounces), along with extra bulbs and batteries and a spare micro light. He carried extra food, rain gear, extra clothes, his favorite trail-running shoes, and a Mylar space blanket (2.5 ounces). Like Reinhold Messner, Orion carried two pairs of glacier sunglasses with side covers and indestructible polycarbonate lenses because he knew that *you won't make it down from the mountains if you end up blind.*

He carried a backpacker's basic first aid kit (1.4 pounds), used for treating everything from blisters and sprains to larger flesh wounds and stocked with over-the-counter medications in anticipation of visceral aches and pain. He carried a Victorinox Swiss Army Explorer knife (4.2 ounces, fully loaded) with its corkscrew, can-opener, scissors, in-line Phillips screwdriver, tweezers, and magnifying glass to find such things as splinters. He carried three boxes of twenty-five windproof, waterproof, stormproof matches—0.65 ounces per box—matches that burn in heavy rain and even while wet; still, he carried a lightweight plastic match-cylinder with a NASA-style O-ring and an emergency fire-starter flint on the cylinder bottom, just in case.

The things he carried were largely determined by practicality. Among the practicalities or near-necessities was the need to maintain a wholesome supply of drinking water—since the water in Nepal was known to be lethal or nearly lethal, depending on the exact nature of the waterborne diseases that are rife. Toward this end, Orion carried plastic water containers and a complete water purification system—1.3 pounds—capable of filtering four liters of sodden tarn through a 0.02-micron hollow fiber membrane purifier to remove suspended particles, protozoa, and bacteria in less than fifteen minutes. What he carried was partly a function of redundancy or overkill, for he also carried pads of cotton filter cloth, packets of calcium hypochlorite, packets of chlorine dioxide, and even iodine tablets, not knowing the actual mechanisms of action of such chemical agents against viruses or any microorganisms, for that matter.

To make certain, he carried a windproof petrochemical camp stove—1.2 pounds—whose integrated heat exchanger, fused to a 1.7-liter pot, completely enclosed the radiant burner and blocked even the most extreme winds, bringing a liter of icy water to a boil in about four minutes. The cunning practicality of this system was based on its simplicity and its multifunctionality, for the strategic addition of some dehydrated food would yield Orion a hot meal in less than ten minutes. In addition to the camp stove itself, he packed a cluster of four fuel canisters–weighing 8 ounces each—a titanium double-wall drinking mug with its integral folding handle—4.2 ounces—and a 0.6-ounce titanium spoon-fork combination known to wilderness backpackers and fast food connoisseurs as a *spork*.

He carried the emotional baggage of a man who knew that he might come home empty-handed, that terrible weight of loving and longing, and an onerous grief tinged with misery and a fear that bordered on horror—yes, *the horror*—that dreadful and repugnant monstrosity that sneaks up upon the unwary do-gooder and drags him down, down, down into the bottomless deep of the abyss, that malignant thing that has plagued mankind since time began, that thing that maws and mutilates our race, not killing us outright, but letting us live on with half a heart and less than half a brain.

Because he knew one could fall and die quickly from so many circumstances found at the high elevations, he carried a modicum of climbing protection. He packed a pair of telescoping carbon-fiber trekking poles—13.5 ounces—and a pair of razor-sharp, strap-on crampons—1.9 pounds—designed for general mountaineering techniques and to work well with the new stiff-sole, full-grain leather hiking boots that he was breaking in. He carried an aluminum-alloy ice axe—1.3 pounds—with a steel head and adjustable leash for routine glissading and occasional self-arrest to prevent freefalling. To protect himself and his packs from the unforgiving sharpness of both the crampons and the ice axe, Orion had carefully fitted thermoplastic point protectors onto the tips of each of the precipitous cusps in a discerning act of preemptive prophylaxis.

What he carried was partly a function of preference, and partly of field experience. As a longtime member of the National Ski Patrol, Orion knew that a definitive "belt" or body harness was of fundamental importance to himself and the alpine search and rescue teams. In most cases, he would be expected to carry his own personal climbing ropes for use on mountain rescues, his favorite being a hefty 11mm x 60m dynamic kernmantle-style rope rated for fifteen falls and weighing more than ten pounds, which together with a basic rack of slings, carabiners, cordelettes, anchors, pegs, hammer, wired nuts, hexentrics, belay devices, and extractor tools for the climbing gear, not to mention a helmet, added another seventeen pounds, minimum. After deliberating the gravity of the situation versus the total weight of the many things he carried, Orion opted for the barest of necessities: that being a micro rappel system neatly contained in a ballistic nylon deployment bag with its convertible belt/harness, minimal descender, single pair of carabiners, and thirty meters of tenuous 5mm tech cord—weighing only 2.7 pounds, period.

For the most part, he carried himself with quiet dignity, maintaining an aloof and perceptibly athletic poise of mind and body language that comes or rather goes with the territory. Orion strived above all to maintain an air of lofty ambition; however, now and then there were moments of strenuous doubt. There were moments when he would reflect upon the perceived hollowness of his existence, in the context of current events, and he would begin to doubt the premises upon which the entire firmament was based in the midst of such dreadful, earth-shattering uncertainties. He carried a new, secret doubt that things might not always be as they seemed on the surface, that things might not always be in accordance with his training and the overly practiced simplicity of his determined yet uncomplicated mind. He dreaded the thought that he might be deceived by anyone, let alone his beloved Überjoy, and so he struggled to keep this secret doubt unquestionably restrained. Nonetheless, in spite of his efforts, he now carried the hero's greatest fear, which is the fear of being unloved. By and large, he carried such dreadful things on the inside, maintaining a mask of intrepidity and a posture of supreme confidence.

As a serviceable carry-on for his journey to Nepal, Orion carried a North Face daypack filled with extra socks and clothes and food and toilet paper and various personal items gathered in a blur from the singular sporting goods store, the hotel bathroom, and the slew of airport concession stands. Among the packages of trail-mix, salted nuts, granola bars, chewing gum, ear buds, nail files, tiny bars of soap, bottled water, plastic lighters, disposable razors, medicinal remedies, and six fluid ounces of insect repellent that he packed into the copious pockets of the daypack, only the disposable razors were summarily forfeited at the airport security checkpoint, which was functioning aggressively if imperfectly in this post-9/11 era. Orion knew that his personal hygiene would have to be catch-as-catch-can from here on out. Still, he carried money—much of his available savings—for he reasoned that American dollars might serve him well, in lieu of adequate preparation, moral edification, and even personal hygiene, if truth be told.

Secreted deep within the innermost pocket of his overstuffed daypack, which lay firmly ensconced in the overhead luggage compartment, close within his reach, was a crimson thong—her crimson thong—and, of all the things he thoughtfully carried, it was the thing that now mattered to him most. For it carried her flaming sensuality, her consummate femininity, her stage-worthy sense of style, and even her remarkable smell. What's more, it carried with it one of Orion's fondest of all memories: the kind of lingering memories that eternally recurrent dreams are made of. Visions of a woman in a ravishing red evening gown moving slowly with an unspoken appeal that turns all heads in her direction, turns all masculine thoughts to the elegant halter neckline which flows to a V-neck bodice that defines the bust perfectly, to the line of eye-catching rhinestones descending along each side of the beautiful fitted bodice that hugs the waist and hips and then falls fully to the ground with lavish appeal as she turns and passes and the pleasing contours of her back are enhanced by the thick, crisscross straps that form a lovely V-shape above the buttocks, a lovely V-shaped insinuation above the crimson thong.

As the 747 jumbo jet rose to its cruising altitude and extended its course along the enormity of a great navigational arc, one that would carry him ever so progressively over the shadowy contours of the seemingly benighted world, Orion retrieved the crimson thong from the overhead compartment with practiced nonchalance. He adjusted his business-class seat into a fully reclined position, covered himself with the gossamer veil of an airline blanket, and breathed in the pleasing redolence of their solely begotten love.

It always seemed to him like a dream within a dream, with time moving slowly, steadily in one direction—away—while this treasured memory was moving in the other, moving toward him; not fading when the nightfall comes upon him like a silent shroud of taffeta, but pressing in upon his fretful slumber with a warm, soft kiss, ripening in the marrow of his mind until she is resting comfortably in his arms again. It was the night of the senior prom when her unnerving beauty danced his formative universe into existence. Moving upon the earth like a celestial dignitary who inhabits a world all her own, she danced like moonlight that plays upon the shadows of the statues in the parks, animating the stillness of the entire landscape with her romance and intrigue, ennobling everyday life with her sweet, angelic presence that moved and breathed like the winds of the heavens upon all the creatures of the earth. Oh, what a joy to behold.

With anxious anticipation, Orion had made careful preparations for this particular night, and he was feeling lucky. He was feeling lucky when he managed to borrow his parent's Chevy Blazer for the evening. His ostensible purpose was to ferry more friends to the dance, but his real goal was one of latent sexual intimacy. He was feeling lucky when he secretly packed the foam pads and sleeping bags into the rear compartment of the Blazer. He was feeling lucky from the first moment he saw her in that crimson evening gown, with her hair plaited like spun gold and knotted with blood red ribbons; lucky from the first moment she moved and breathed and smiled and spoke to him at the threshold of eternity. He was feeling lucky when he managed to dance each of those special slow dances with this magnificent woman of the world who would now and forevermore come to him in his dreams. And he *was* lucky, for she was with him and him alone, every step of the way.

It was a sensual summer night—a night when fresh currents of expectation arouse the senses, and innuendo as delicate as a midnight breeze blows soft and warm upon the mind, when the road through a moistening woodland is seen as a river of moonlight that flows on and on and leads young lovers to an enchanted lake deep in a softwood forest filled with aromatic cedars, pines, and firs. It was an eventful summer night—a night when a queen among the angels is crowned with her lover's adoration, when bright eyes sparkle with immutable promise, each in their own jeweled sky. It was a blissful summer night—a night when a sovereign beauty invites one particular man into the sacrosanct chamber of her coronation, when untapped wineskins are inexorably opened and common bedding becomes a purple moor.

Orion was pretty sure that he is dreaming now, and he was—that same dream within a dream—and she is rising up to meet him as he opens up his eyes. The world is moving and she is right there with him, and they are together again, as if they are floating high above it, and they are drifting through the forest, and she is taking off her dress, and they are moving very slowly, gliding just above the turf. The world is moving and she is dancing seminaked in the moonlight, and they are staring at each other like they are floating on the waters, moving out in all directions, and he feels a pleasant elevation as her hands are moving slowly, and she loosens up his belt. The world is moving and Orion is sure that she is embracing him, as she was, enveloping and tenderly possessing him, as she was.

The dream continues on as lovely eyes shut, flushed cheeks burn, and full lips caress most strident flesh, slowly, softly, almost rhythmically, while the gentle susurrations of the towering evergreen trees appear to undulate in unison and occasionally moan out loud with the winsome transit of the moistening breezes. The urgency of unrequited bliss swells within him again and again as Orion struggles to maintain a semblance of composure. Gazing intently at this elegant swan-like creature, who has wafted in like mist from some enchanted lake unto his bailiwick where yellow pears hang overripened on the vine, he is amazed by this pleasing manifestation of femininity who now moves at will upon his quavering flanks with such fluidic insinuations as to make him tremble, her near-nakedness gleaming in the moonlight like an ethereal work of art carved by nature's consummate beauty in flawless alabaster. This graceful, swan-like woman, now drunk with siphoned kisses and filled with wild roses, bends her limber neck and dips her exquisite head beneath the guiding pressures of his trembling hands. When she rises to her feet, the couple walks hand in hand across the most beautiful bridge in the world of dreams to a waiting love nest that is literally brimming with gossamer down.

At first, they spoke not a word, for the language of the young lovers was composed in the breathless silence of pure desire punctuated by ardent kisses, by searching tongues, by quaking heaves of mounting pleasures at once revealed and lavishly expressed. An ambrosial fragrance of intoxication issued, it seemed, from every pore, pooling in hidden places that were longing to be discovered and then fervently explored. Orion was keenly enamored of Joycelyn's pink and alabaster breasts, which nearly drove him mad with yearning for their pliant, sumptuous magnitudes and circular geometries of outstanding perfection. Her glistening thighs, both smooth and warm, were gradually parted under the onslaught of his persistent caresses, yielding a satin mound of lush crimson that shone in the dim evening light with a faint ethereal gleam all its own, as if the satin wedge of fabric was not merely reflecting the moonlight that poured in through the windows but was itself issuing a discernable radiance from glimmering embers that burned with desire beneath the shapely surface. The delicate and alluring crimson mound of the thong spurred Orion on to such concupiscence that the satin fabric was soon soaked to a dripping wetness from the strivings of his perfervid kisses.

Time spent at the very gates of paradise passes with a cadence all its own, and at this juncture in the recurrent dream, Orion was more inclined to thoroughly please his beloved than to have his own passions fulfilled at her expense. Nevertheless, Joycelyn's seminude body began to arch toward the heavens and to surge with a series of powerful muscular undulations as Orion continued to apply the instruments of oral assertiveness to the very source of her newfound urgency. Her rising spasms increased to such an extent that Orion began to worry whether or not he was quite possibly hurting her, and he was about to cease his deluge of tender, wet kisses upon her heaving mound when she cried out with the voice of an angel those words that would forever fill his cosmic void:

"I want you!" she said in the moonlight. "I want you!" Her voice echoed into the night. "I want you now and forever!" she cried out. "I want you with all of my might!"

Orion would never know if Joycelyn's expressions of impassioned desire were somehow practiced or prepared for him, or whether they amounted to a more spontaneous form of prose. All he knew of these amorous words—which were repeated oh, so often in the enchanted realm of his lingering dreams—was that her aspiring body was the *Whole of Art* to his youthfully innocent eyes, and that her ecstatic voice was the *Whole of Poetry* to his relatively unsophisticated ears.

And then they were naked, her sumptuous velveteen surfaces moving upon his masculine mantle as a warm blush passes unseen over amorous faces, spreading over their corporeal bodies as sensuous tongues of flame that warm the blood to the point where bare skin breaks out into a gentle lubricating sweat like tiny tears of joy that arise in a wave of seraphic contemplation that reaches out beyond what the mind understands with a fervency of will that coalesces the soul and extends itself toward the object of its desire to the emphatic precipice with a crystalline dew that drips tenderly from one open heart to another. And then, just as she is guiding the torch of his most preeminent inclination into the luscious proclivity of her very own desire, Orion finds himself drawn away from the scene, above and away from the erotic couple that was just a moment ago rapt in heaven's guileless jubilation.

Perhaps something deep within him forbade the heartwarming recollection, not wanting to tarnish the precious memory, not wanting to cheapen the exalted experience by vulgar repetition. He knew not why, but it was always the same. Frustration mounted as he attempted to reimmerse and reorient his dreaming brain back to the lake and the swan, back to the impassioned warmth of her embrace, back to the mesmerizing romance of her charismatic presence and the innocence of their bare, naked bliss. But, alas, it was always the same. He found himself alone in a dark, dank cavern, attracted and allured by a myriad of copulating bodies, wanting in some strange manner to be born again in her arms, only to be censured by some unnamed prohibition that warned him he would surely lose her forever if he lingered there too long. By then, Orion was wide awake, aware once again that the entire world is woefully deficient, and that the only thing for him to do is to strive and to persevere as he yearns for his dream of beauty to return.

As the 747 jumbo jet descended from the lofty purview of its cruising altitude to prepare for its scheduled landing in Hong Kong, en route to Kathmandu, Orion gazed wistfully out the window of the plane and peered down at the specks of earth moving beneath the clouds. He was descending all right—he was beginning to separate that which was real from that which could only be imagined. He touched the thong, which he'd now pocketed, with his fingertips, and he began to sink into a feeling of hopelessness given the enormity of the task at hand. Dislocated from the enchanted forest of his recurrent reveries, Orion was left alone with conflicting impressions of his namesake. Is it Orion the great hunter, the violent and conquering hero, who stands poised eternally to *strike* at a moment's notice? Or, rather, is it Orion the grief-stricken lover who can be viewed as reaching somewhat more sublimely into the heavens—reaching out to his beloved who is fading faintly into darkness like the whiteness of swans or the piteousness of lost doves or the wake of so many generations of lost children who are fading as faintly as the Pleiades, which move evermore into the vast emptiness beyond his reach.

3. Et Tu, Kathmandu?

A *reversal of thrust* is a phrase loaded with rhetorical, literary, even theatrical connotations, and all of the above could be applied to the dramatic situation at hand. However, for the time being, the reversal of thrust may refer more precisely to the mechanical redirection of the jet blasts emanating from the powerful Rolls-Royce engines of the Dragonair 320 Airbus—a thrust that was effectuated upon its landing at the international airport in Kathmandu—propelling Orion abruptly forward to the impending edge of his adventure.

It was going on 11:00 p.m. when Orion cleared customs, as it were, changed some US dollars into wads of Nepalese rupees, shouldered his expedition pack, daypack, and overstuffed duffle bag, and headed out of the airport terminal—out into the incipient darkness and a fog that was thickly laced with the ambience of exhaust fumes, wood smoke, wisps of temple incense, vague, unrecognizable spices, and a throat-closing miasma of burning tires, and, worse, of cremated bodies. He noticed that the prevailing murkiness of the nighttime was made more salient by the observation that there were few, if any, streetlights in the foreground, and that those situated near the entrance of the airport terminal were not working at the time. The only light to see by was coming vaguely through the glass windows of the red brick terminal itself or from the transient glare of some departing motorcars, each of which seemed to be struggling with some inscrutable antagonistic obstacle in the oppressive darkness before finally managing to gain sufficient driving speed to escape for a few determined moments of travel, only to disappear altogether into the distance and the far-reaching shroud of night.

Orion adjusted his perceptions to the dimness and the fog, and he began to notice the presence of a small horde of people who were approaching him from out of the nebulous gloom, a gloom which made all things appear more mysterious and grotesque. When the figures drew nearer, he could tell that they were simply men, not threatening but strange and disheveled in appearance, men whose eyes glinted in the surrounding darkness, men whose clothing might be construed as some form of poverty but whose facial expressions were uniformly that of helpfulness tinged with expectation. *Of course,* he thought to himself, *they are offering to help me carry my bags ... perhaps to a nearby taxi stand, perhaps to the hotel ... but which hotel ... which one to choose?*

Orion began to realize that he had indeed prepared himself for a journey in the wilderness and, admittedly, hadn't given much thought to this particular "tomorrow," as suggested by the cryptic message he received from the Seven Sisters and Company—he had chosen instead to spend his time reminiscing and dreaming moistly and then sleeping in the illusory arms of his beloved Überjoy. Yes, indeed, he had sought out the kingdom; that is, if said kingdom referred to the Kingdom of Nepal. *So far so good,* he thought, *but what to do now? And with whom to go, and to where?*

The disheveled cluster of Nepalese porters and taxi drivers and helpful guides continued to assemble and converge upon the upright figure of the American adventurer, whilst the would-be hero began to realize that *the casting of pearls, the sounding of trumpets,* and *the narrowness of gates* seemed, at this very moment, a bit too obscure to be of any immediate practicality or even guidance to him. Orion attempted to skirt the issue by moving decisively away from the local welcoming committee to another equally tenebrous location under another unilluminated streetlamp. He was followed by an even greater number of polite yet persistent luggage assistants, whose offers of helpfulness, worldly advice, vast experience, and superior wisdom was not diminished in the least but appeared to be magnified by the observation that their entreaties were delivered largely by imploring facial expressions, confident hand gestures, and mere snippets of broken English. Orion was unnerved and somewhat frustrated—not by the gregarious offers from these curious people who remained half-hidden in the darkness, for he was much more alarmed by his own state of indecision than he was by the crush of the men with the glinting eyes, the grinning faces, the sea of outstretched hands that were earnestly gesturing for his attention as they eagerly groped for his belongings.

As his widening eyes continued to adjust to the caliginous mise-en-scène, Orion raised his gaze above the clamor to the nearby parking area, where he saw more shadowy figures arrayed among an unorganized sprawl of tiny motor vehicles, each one only slightly larger than a conveyance a Westerner might expect to find at a children's amusement park. He was considering the sheer possibility and the logistics of cramming his sturdy frame into one of these diminutive motor vehicles when he felt a forceful hand upon his shoulder, and he turned to face a man nearly as tall as himself.

"Are you ready to hunt some bad guys?" said the man without further introduction.

"As ready as I'll ever be," said Orion, stroking back his hair in reflex, for he was somewhat taken aback by the sudden appearance of this mysterious stranger who seemed to materialize out of nowhere. He studied the lion-like face of the man in the low-key lighting, as it were. The face was sunburned bronze—the kind of intense, ruddy tan one finds at high altitudes on ski instructors and mountaineering guides—but the comportment of the man was hardly that of an instructor or a guide. There was not even the slightest hint of a smile that might have been congruent with his opening remark. Apparently, there was no implicit cordiality or even civility in the expression of the question, just an overbearing mantle of seriousness and a snarling glint of metal among the tobacco-stained teeth. The eyes were cold, expressionless eyes that might have been blue, Orion guessed, or they might have been green, for in the diminished light outside the airport terminal, the man's face was still shadowy and severe. The eyes, devoid of specificity of color, were cold and hard and sharp like fractured glass.

The eyes of the man in the incipient darkness and the fog were unlike the eyes of the assembled horde of porters and taxi drivers, eyes which were uniformly open and expressive, eyes lacking entirely in malevolence, eyes that were instructive and expectant, almost pleading in a calm and abiding manner. The cold, hard, predatory eyes of the austere man in the incipient darkness and the fog were unlike the eyes of Orion himself; that is, the keen, earnest, and discerning eyes of the lonely hunter whose outward actions cannot help but demonstrate the native act and figure of his outwardly aching heart, and whose steady gaze is but a complement to his own internal quest for love and duty that is so openly worn upon his sleeve as to invite the feathered phantoms of the benighted world to peck the very light from his aspiring orbs. Conversely, the eyes of fractured glass were the unremitting eyes of a killer, to be sure, a killer who sees the world through its many shattered windshields; a killer who peers through two empty holes where bullets have passed cleanly through a plate glass window without shattering anything but the small, surrounding circles; a killer who looks at you as though he would rather be sizing up the entire world through the Mil-Dot reticle of a high-powered rifle, if he weren't already. Their eyes met—the hunter and the killer—their eyes met in a moment of complete understanding.

"I'm ready to go anywhere," said Orion finally. "I'm ready to do whatever needs to be done."

"Good. That's what I needed to hear," the man said, offering Orion his hand. "They told me you were a hard case … and I'm glad about that." The handshake was obviously some kind of signal, for as soon as the universal act of accord was completed, two bright headlights flashed on in the foreground, and the distinctive sound of a Land Rover Defender engine was heard approaching them from out of the dim. "Stay hard, hunter," said the man as he opened the tailgate of the Land Rover for Orion to load in his gear. "That's the only way you stand even half a chance of being successful."

They drove in silence away from the international airport terminal into a greater darkness, led solely, it appeared, by the high-beam headlights of the Land Rover that cut like a pair of glowing scissors through the obscurity, reaching out and probing the superficial firmament of the paved road ahead, veering widely around the unmarked obstacles, jarring potholes, and occasional pedestrians seen manhandling heavily burdened bicycles along the shoulder; the Land Rover's beams cut through the darkness while probing for the undefined midpoint of the macadam in a nervous effort to avoid impending dangers that loomed beyond the margins of the pavement. Orion could make out the features of some strange, unlit buildings in the periphery and the shapes of indeterminate figures moving slowly like ghostly shadows that passed by his window in the gloom of night.

"Looks like another blackout in the city," said the leonine man with the killer's eyes. "Take the Kamal Pokhari to Durbar Marg," he said to the Nepali driver, who nodded without turning his head.

They passed a cement building with dull yellow flames and black smoke streaming out through ruptured doors and windows, and what appeared to be several bodies covered with blankets in the foreground. Then darkness returned to their surroundings, and the high-beam scissors again reached out for the road ahead.

They drove on without speaking, making their way up a gradual rise in the terrain until they crested the rim of a hill at the approach of an immense semicircular valley. There, spread out before them, was the sprawling capital city of Kathmandu, cloaked in a mysterious uniformity of darkness that was broken here and there by sporadic clusters of electric lights in the distance, which served only to reveal the full expanse of the power outage afflicting the low-rise metropolis. Beyond the sprawl of the Kathmandu Valley loomed the pitch-black wall of Himalayas to the north, embracing the scene like an ancient theater whose proscenium arch was formed by the illusory bend of the heavens—heavens that shone tonight through parting clouds as a shade of stars and midnight blue.

"That's what happens when you blow up the power stations," said the leonine man with eyes like fractured glass to Orion. "Not to mention the public works buildings."

"What, exactly, is happening?" asked Orion.

"They're supposedly conserving energy … with rotating blackouts and load-shedding schedules throughout the various districts. But lately it's just *turn off the power and go home to bed.*"

"I mean with the bombings," said Orion. "What do the Maoists expect to accomplish by turning off the lights?"

"Ah, that's when the real mischief starts," said the leonine man, looking out the side window. "See over there …" he added, pointing to a dull glow off in the distance. "That used to be a government installation, a revenue office, as I recall. I guess they didn't find enough rupees in the banks they robbed last week."

"Guess not," said Orion in amazement as he leaned over to see. "Can't the local police do anything to stop the lawlessness before it gets out of hand?"

"That building we passed a ways back—the one with the fire coming out of the windows—that *was* a local police station."

"So much for law and order," said Orion, "I guess we're in the thick of it."

"As thick as it gets," said the man with the eyes like fractured glass. "And in case you were wondering what kind of danger you're in for … you can be sure they stripped all the guns from the lockers and the dead bodies before they burned the place to the ground."

They drove on through the ramshackle streets of the city, where they encountered a dense congestion of cars and trucks and a weave of muttering motorcycles, each issuing a dim light, at best, as they flashed by along the continuous rows of houses and storefronts, all of which were closed for business at that time of night. Orion began to roll down the window, only to find his sensibilities confronted by an immediate tumult of harsh traffic noises and the acrid smell and taste of diesel fumes tinctured with a nauseating amalgam of cooking fires, sandalwood incense, garbage, and human waste. He slowly, decisively rolled the window back up.

"The bombings come with demands for general strikes to further their cause ... and then they target any public services, stores, and businesses that fail to comply," said the killer, speaking directly to Orion. "Eventually, everyone learns to comply," he added.

Orion simply nodded.

"Damn commies!" exclaimed the man. "They even bombed the Coca-Cola factory! And *that* I just can't understand. You know, I get the guns and the money. I get the politics and the mentality of violence and terror—" He stopped abruptly in midsentence, as though he were suddenly contemplating the ramifications of some deep philosophical question. And then he added, "Who doesn't like Coca-Cola?"

The Land Rover came to a halt at the Yak and Yeti, a hotel complex located at the virtual center of Kathmandu in the historic district of the Royal Palace, where dynastic mullahs and shah kings ruled the roost for hundreds of years, and where a single disenchanted prince could change the course of history in the wink of an eye. Orion was ushered away from the welcoming porte-cochere of the hotel lobby along a path of dark emerald gardens with gurgling stone fountains that flowed like a solemn mystery into the depths of an impenetrable lotus pond. He passed a succession of increasingly antiquated Nepali architectural elements to the entrance of the Lal Durbar, an ornate neoclassical Rana palace, which stood in opulent contrast to the adjacent buildings' concrete facades. Entering by way of a royal corridor lined with huge gilt mirrors and decked with marble that had been imported from Italy and transported through India on the backs of many long-departed porters, they arrived at the entrance of a grand dining room illuminated by ornate chandeliers that hung from the vaulted ceilings like celestial constellations. The walls were covered with elaborate, gilded woodwork enveloping elegant antique mirrors, priceless murals, and portraits of the royal descendants of Jung Bahadur Rana, an army general who had usurped power from the monarchy in the 1800s and established himself as the prime minister and supreme maharaja, claiming absolute authority superior to that of any sovereign. Seated at a single linen-covered table in the very center of the spacious dining room was a pale and curious-looking man in white silk pajamas. He was being served what appeared to be breakfast by a Nepalese man wearing a white linen shirt and a bright red vest.

"Delivering one American hero, still wet behind the ears and hugely uninformed, sir," said the man with eyes like fractured-glass, whose severe, leonine features contorted into a perplexing configuration that could almost be mistaken for a smile.

"Thank you, colonel," said the man in the silk pajamas, who stopped sawing his ham steak just long enough to size up Orion, who immediately noticed that the curious-looking man's deep-set eyes were distinctively crossed to such an extent that it made direct eye contact somewhat problematic. "He looks sturdy enough to me," said the man, stuffing a large bolus of ham into his mouth. "The only question I have," he added while still chewing, "is whether or not this man has the constitution for the mission at hand ... a mission that will harden the heart ... a mission that will try the temper ... a mission that will assuredly hurt like the dickens before it is over."

Orion looked over at the leonine killer and apparent *colonel* of a yet undisclosed organization, who was presently fixing himself a drink at a bar in front of a large framed glass mirror. He appeared in reflection to be staring with contempt into a vintage tumbler of Scotch whiskey as though he were gazing at a cadre of prehistoric insects trapped in a circular glob of amber, frozen in lugubrious space and time, helpless to resist the thickening oppressiveness of some vague and eternal present. And then he emptied the contents of the glass in one swift motion and stared blankly into the mirrored glass.

Orion felt increasingly uncomfortable, standing alone at the entrance of the opulent dining room, having neither been invited in nor addressed directly, let alone offered either food or drink by his ungracious hosts. He tried to recall the specifics of his previous instructions, as indefinite as they now seemed to be, and then he suddenly stepped forward and made a bold series of declarative announcements.

"My name is a pearl that I will keep to myself. My business is private and personal. I am only interested in helicopter trekking. And now that I have obviously found the kingdom, I am looking to book a flight with Fishtail Air, Limited."

An eerie silence filled the mirrored room, and all eyes focused on Orion.

"That will be all, Gunga," said the man in the white silk pajamas to the man in the bright red vest. And then he silently motioned for Orion to approach the table while the servant left the room, carefully closing the great oaken doors behind him.

"It appears that our hunter is not as naïve as he looks," said the pale man in the white silk pajamas.

"That's my impression also," said the colonel, still viewing the scene indirectly through its reflections in the mirror.

"Then our hunter may imagine that he is definitely not in the office of the US Consulate, as is the general custom when one registers and embarks upon a private trekking expedition. He is definitely not to be given official permission to stray off the beaten paths into any unauthorized or restricted territories. And he is fully aware that neither the US government nor the Geneva Conventions will be of any help to him, should he find himself involved in any—shall I say—unfortunate altercations with the indigenous fauna."

As he spoke, the man in the white silk pajamas did not look up from his plate, except to sip some coffee from a bone china cup. And then, stuffing the last remnants of poached eggs and ham onto his fork with a soggy shred of toast, he added, "And although the present king has given explicit permissions for authorized personnel to bring certain rebel leaders to justice—that is, they are *Wanted Dead or Alive*—no such permissions or rewards are to be expected from anyone involved in said helicopter trekking."

Before Orion could answer for himself, the colonel quickly replied, "I'll make sure that he fully understands the rules, sir."

"Well, then, it looks like my breakfast is finished."

Orion tried and failed to make any kind of eye contact with the man in the white silk pajamas, who now rose from the table and exited the room as though no one else were present, like a maharaja who remains utterly aloof, a supreme lord of all he surveys.

The sky was brightening with the dawn as the Land Rover Defender made its way among a crush of traffic through the historic district of Thamel, passing Durbar Square with its vast conglomerations of medieval architecture and stone temples and shrines of every denomination, with sacred altars and ornamental flowers and filth coexisting in the same seedy squalor as the dirt-poor inhabitants of the sprawling capital city.

"I want to thank you for vouching for me back there," said Orion. "I'm playing for keeps, and I don't care how many mountains I have to move."

"Just keep your head about you, hunter. A guy like you might turn out to be the last man standing ... with a little help from your brothers and sisters, that is."

"If I understand correctly, I'll be trekking in relative darkness ... even darker than dark—almost black. Is that why I wasn't introduced?"

"It's hard to have a conversation with someone you haven't even met," said the colonel. "You have something more valuable than permission ... you have deniability."

"Understood," said Orion, looking out the window at the assemblage of porters and vendors setting up shop in the early morning hours. "So, how will I recognize my brothers and sisters in this strange land?"

"Your family is much like *black ice*. By the time you begin to figure that out, it would be too late."

"So, you're saying they'll find me."

"Something like that." As he spoke, the colonel's glasslike eyes squinted to a sharp focus upon a steep, tree-covered hillside rising high above the roadway at the northwestern limits of the Kathmandu Valley. The driver steered the Land Rover off the pavement at the base of the mountain. "See that brightly painted gateway and those stairs beyond it?"

"I see them," said Orion. "Several hundred steps, I reckon."

"Let's see how fast you can carry *one* of your packs up those steps," said the colonel, emphasizing the word *one*. "As if someone's life depends on it," he added.

Orion grabbed a midweight parka from his daypack and quickly put it on, followed by his hefty Baltoro expedition pack. Then he grabbed a bottle of water, pocketed some energy bars, placed one shiny red thong into his innermost pocket, and headed through a narrow gate and up the stone steps in a hurry, leaving the daypack and the duffle bag and the leering leonine colonel behind.

The ancient stairway led Orion up the base of the mountain. Large golden statues of Buddha sitting serenely flanked both sides of the ancient path, which rose sharply up the mountain on steepening steps well-worn by countless pilgrimages over two millennia, ascending further up between pairs of iconic statues of peacocks, horses, elephants, lions, and Garudas, the large, mythical protector-birds combining the characteristics of eagles and divine beings, sworn enemies of the serpents and dragons they are characteristically known to hunt. Working hard to maintain a good pace with the weight of his expedition pack upon him, Orion's leg muscles burned fiercely with battery acid, and his masculine heart pumped furiously with oxygenated blood and desire—desire to begin, desire to ascend, desire to have and to hold her divine embodiment once again.

He continued to climb relentlessly, barely aware of the swarms of temple monkeys that were scampering just out of his way or of the lines of early morning pilgrims who moved with a slow cadence of devotion, each contemplative thought an affirmation of tradition, each undistracted step a defeat of Mara (wicked distraction) with a confident and resounding *touch* upon the earth.

Orion cleared the top of the stairway, breathless and panting. He stumbled upon a garish stone lion guarding the entrance of the temple mound and, clutching for his balance, he raised his gaze upward to the profusion of prayer flags strung overhead in graceful lines from spires and trees, fluttering in the morning breeze like a chorus of inanimate angels, adding pure hues of elemental colors and a general impression of lightness to the overarching canopy. Suddenly, Orion was stunned by an uncanny feeling bordering on astonishment as he gazed up at the unblinking eyes of Buddha painted in vivid colors upon the surface of a bright, aurous face. He was immediately struck by a sense of awe, followed by a quivering sense of awareness that spread like static electricity over his body, followed by a gathering sense of calm that reminded him of snowflakes falling faintly through the darkness on a cold and windless night.

He followed a group of red-robed monks to the left as they circumambulated the great domed monument, or *stupa*, moving calmly in a purposeful clockwise direction, spinning periodic arrays of prayer wheels as they went along. Above the lofty whitewashed dome stood a golden cuboidal structure, upon which the watchful eyes of the primordial Buddha looked out in all directions, and above the golden cube extended a succession of gilded tiers that formed a spire from which long lines of prayer flags radiated. It was barely eight o'clock. The sun had risen fully and was burning through the morning mists, softly illuminating a myriad of smaller stupas, temples, and votive shrines in the foreground, revealing the full extent of the valley before him, the green flanks of the wooded foothills, and the snow-covered peaks of the great Himalayas that rose above and beyond all imagining.

Orion barely noticed the artful stone *chaityas* and golden shrines depicting the "immovable one" in various aspects of enlightened consciousness, and he ignored the pilgrims in prostration showing reverence to the "triple gem"; he was searching for something more tangible, something in particular, something recognizable, perhaps, as a friend. His attention was drawn to a Nepali man in an orange sweatshirt sitting on the open ground beside a pagoda-style temple.

There were wire cages of bright green and yellow parakeets beside him, and he seemed to be gesturing for Orion to come and speak with him. This proved to be somewhat difficult, for the man was speaking Nepali Bhasa, a Newari dialect, and in spite of the most earnest and exaggerated discourse, along with beseeching animation and sweeping hand gestures, Orion soon became frustrated and abandoned all communications.

"He wants you to purchase one of the birds," said a young man in perfect English. He appeared to have been drawn to the scene by the commotion. His skin was the color of autumn wheat, and the disheveled condition of his filthy clothing, worn down to threadbare rags, was incongruent with the obvious precision of his diction.

"What do I want with a bird?" replied Orion, eyeing the raggedy translator with suspicion.

"He wants you to purchase one of the birds, sahib, in an effort to set it free."

The symbolic connotations of the situation at hand were not lost on Orion, who promptly dug into one of the pockets of his expedition pack and produced an American ten-dollar bill. Thinking he could use all the so-called karma he could get, Orion handed the bill to the birdman, and then he spoke directly to the raggedy translator: "Tell him to keep the change."

Seemingly pleased with the financial transaction, the birdman opened a small door in one of the cages and proceeded to release the colorful birds one by one. Immediately upon their release, each bird flew up and away and disappeared into the multicolored canopy. Orion shouldered his pack and walked with determination over to a low stone wall at the edge of the temple complex. He looked beyond the present confines to the far-reaching metropolis of Kathmandu and further up into the foothills. There were eagles passing overhead, soaring in slow, resolute arcs; there were pigeons feeding off old stone floors, and many were roosting comfortably in the safety of ancient temple shrines.

"You *do* realize that those birds are simply going to fly back into those same cages," said the shabby translator, who had followed behind Orion. By then, though, the would-be hero's mind was too far afield; his thoughts were too far gone into the distant vistas and the mountains to be concerned with the psychology of birds.

"You *do* realize that those birds are simply going to fly back—"

"I heard you the first time," said Orion, not at all pleased with the interruption. "I don't have time to worry about things like that. I'm here to find something valuable for myself ... something more objective!"

"The teachings of the enlightened one suggest that it might be better for you to view the world without objective referent," replied the persistent man in the raggedy clothes.

"All I know is that every day that I sit on my ass and think about it is a day that I lose!" Orion's voice trembled, and his eyes blazed with righteous indignation at the audacity of this raggedy man.

"I am just the translator, sahib ... just a humble servant attempting to point you in the right direction." The man sounded like he was deeply disappointed, and he simply turned and walked away from Orion.

Standing alone again, Orion searched for a friendly face among the milling throngs. There was nothing he could make out, nothing he could recognize as familiar; there was simply nothing and no one in sight. A wave of panic overcame him as Orion began to realize that he blew it! That he had somehow failed some great metaphysical test! He grabbed his pack and took off after the raggedy man with the perfect diction. He found him descending the steps of a landing that led to a large circular stone fountain. In the center of the fountain was a life-size figure standing and smiling with its right hand slightly raised; at its base was a golden globe upon which the words "World Peace" were inscribed in both English and Nepalese. The man continued walking as Orion approached him.

"Did I say something wrong?" asked Orion.

The man continued walking.

"Did I miss some mystical opportunity or fail to speak the right password?"

The man turned briefly, gave him a look of stern disapproval, and then continued on.

Orion followed the raggedy man past the fountain, for lack of a better lead, and he was somewhat surprised to find a parking lot filled with waiting taxis at the western side of the temple complex, considering all the upward steps that he previously had to climb.

At this point, the raggedy man approached one of the waiting taxis and opened the door for Orion. "I'm sorry for any misunderstanding, but I am convinced that it would be best for you to head directly back to the airport," he said, and then he reached inside the front window, handed the driver what appeared to be paper money, and walked away.

Orion looked around several times and then, for lack of anything else to go on, slid his pack and then himself into the backseat of the tiny automobile. His mind reeled at the thought that his hero's journey had come to an end before it had even begun. Lamentations poured from his heart as they drove away in silence. *No!* his mind cried. He wanted to protest out loud, to beg the driver to turn around. His mind raced. Surely, they could go back; surely, he could convince the translator that he had the right answer after all. *Think,* he told himself, forcing his mind to calm. *What should I have said?* He tried to search the corners of his mind and heart for the proper interaction that would have led him on a different course, not this one along which the silent taxi was now descending—descending from the promise and expectation of the sacred temple, descending into the harsh traffic and congestion of the bleak capital city, descending down toward the oily tarmac of the airport that represented nothing but failure. Orion was filled with a penetrating sense of hopelessness and despair that was very nearly inconsolable.

"Don't worry, sahib," said the driver to Orion. "You are still on the path."

4. Thoughts Unbecoming

O rion was greatly relieved when the taxi drove past the entrance of the Kathmandu International Airport terminal and continued on, eventually pulling into a smaller parking lot in front of a series of dilapidated airplane hangars. The driver escorted Orion through the crowded domestic terminal, avoiding the customary array of document checkpoints, guard dog sniffing, and body frisking with the secretive display of the curious paper money provided by the raggedy man at the monkey temple. Then the driver ushered Orion aboard a DeHavilland DHC-6 Twin Otter that was warming up on the tarmac. Orion tried to tip the driver, who smiled as he refused with a polite turn of his head. Instead, the driver placed a folded leaf of paper money in Orion's hand, very discretely, in the course of their parting handshake. As the Twin Otter revved its engines and taxied onto the runway, Orion unfolded the Nepalese banknote and compared it to the other banknotes in his own wad. There, in place of the portrait of King Birendra wearing a plumed crown, was the engraving of an eagle in profile sitting atop a shield displaying a single multifaceted intelligence star.

The deafening roar of the twin-engine turbines signaled the takeoff of a flight that would carry the American hero skyward into the soaring upheavals of the Himalayas. In a matter of minutes, the lush greenery of the Kathmandu Valley receded into the distance. The plane rose beyond the misty foothills into an ethereal haze, and then beyond that haze into a crystalline high-altitude blue that was punctuated by a sparkling snow-covered colossus of mountain peaks which effectively separates that which truly dares to exist from that which can only be imagined. Viewing the vast panorama approaching him through the frosted windows of the high-wing Twin Otter, Orion felt a sense of wonder, followed by a twinge of apprehension when he realized that the straining aircraft would not surmount these towering mountain peaks but was tracking beneath their summits, tracking along in a groove of deepening, darkening valleys which led further and further into the inordinate mountains. The plane's trajectory eventually dropped down toward the slope of a narrow airstrip perched on the side of one particular mountain, descending rapidly toward an impending, unnerving event that could only be described as a controlled crash landing.

The approach to the Lukla airport is the approach to an astonishingly small ledge of bitumen set up against a towering cliff face. The gray sliver of a narrow runway bisects a tiny village that is literally carved into the side of a mountain that rises far above the flattened terrace, a terrace whose mountainous flanks drop precipitously down into the unseen depths of its fathomless foundations. The approach from the air is to the verge of an upward-sloping airstrip that is harrowing for both pilots and passengers: too low, and the aircraft joins the wreckage of those who came in too low; too high, and again there is no tomorrow, for the looming cliff face allows no second chances.

While the DHC-6 Twin Otter bush plane was specifically designed for takeoff and landing at short-field airports, Orion felt like cheering and clapping when the landing gear finally gained purchase and the aircraft, with the help of the extreme slope of the runway, slowed down in a hurry. At the upper end of the runway, the plane taxied to the right onto a level platform. Disembarking, Orion was greeted there by a stocky, bearded man wearing faded black jeans, a black fleece jacket, a camouflage baseball cap, turned backward, and high-altitude sunglasses that wrapped around his deeply suntanned face.

"Welcome to Shangri-La," said the man as he held out his hand to Orion. "I'm Captain Q. T. Umbrage, as far as you're concerned, but you can call me Grudge."

"Pleasure," said Orion. "I'm Q. T. Hunter, to those in the know, but otherwise my friends call me Orion."

The captain laughed and shook his head in disbelief, as if he were looking at the strangest, most unlikely aspect of humanity he had seen all day. Then the captain climbed up into the side of the DHC-6, had some words with the pilots, and reappeared carrying a large duffle bag in each hand. Orion and the captain had to duck and move away from the airplane as it swung around on the platform and taxied back onto the now downward-sloping runway. From Orion's perspective, the runway seemed to be impossibly short, with nothing but thin air beyond it.

"I've seen postage stamps with a larger footprint!" shouted Orion over the din of the accelerating engines.

The two men watched the propeller-driven aircraft surge forward, racing downhill against the limits of space and time, gradually gaining speed in an attempt to gain lift before it disappeared off the runway and into the steep valley down below. With less than ten yards to spare, the Twin Otter flattened out just past the vanishing edge, barely rising at all, but continuing on and on, like life itself, as if it were hanging by an invisible thread.

"Your next landing zone is even smaller, and much higher up," said the captain to Orion. "Go and introduce yourself to Segunda, your mountain guide," he said, pointing to a striking Nepali man in a WWII-vintage khaki military sweater who was standing alone in front of a blue-roofed block house, "while I try and get this yak-and-yeti show on the road."

Orion walked over to the smiling Nepali man and introduced himself as Orion. He couldn't help but notice the more striking aspects of the man: his sturdy build, the strong Mongolian stamp upon his features, and, most particularly, a perplexing smile that beamed forth both an impression of confidence and a discernable trace of condescension.

"So you're the one they call upon when there is man's work to be done. The one they call upon to move beyond the boundaries of discretion into those vast expanses above the rooftops into a larger, wider world. And here you are with your brand new Gregory backpack, all bright and shiny clean, kitted out with all the manly accoutrements of high adventure. The mere look of it fills you with excitement and anticipation that you will soon be leaving the lesser blokes behind; lesser people with lesser ambitions who choose to remain safe in the smallness of their houses and villages, afraid to venture out into the gathering storm. To lesser folks like that, you must appear as a ruddy supreme being, some kind of god. And what do you, O Heroic One, expect to gain from your great adventure? Why, the reacquisition of your women folk, of course. What could be more noble a cause? What could be more *historic* ..."

Segunda was still speaking when Orion turned and walked back to Captain Umbrage, who was loading one of the duffle bags into a Bell 206 JetRanger helicopter that was parked on the platform.

"What's with this guy?" asked Orion. "Is he trying to be funny? Does he think that this is a joke?"

"Oh, that's just Segunda," said the captain. "That's just the way he is ... He's a Gurkha, a British soldier in another life ... There is no question about the *sincerity* and the *consistency* of his unique point of view. And he is an excellent guide for you on this particular mission. The only problem you might have from time to time is in discerning the *reliability* of his narration when it comes to philosophical issues of East and West." The captain laughed and clapped Orion on the back as he signaled for Segunda to join them.

"I don't give a hoot about his philosophy," said Orion. "As long as he can help me find my Überjoy, he is welcome to speak at me any way he likes."

And then Orion was airborne again, rising up above the postage stamp of the Lukla airport, at 9,380 feet above sea level, toward the definitive rooftop of the world, higher and higher into the Solu-Khumbu Himal, the land of giants: giants like Lhotse, Everest, and

Ama Dablam rose up above the clouds as if to greet him. Orion was sitting on a bench seat, just behind Segunda and the helicopter pilot, staring out through the two curved windshields at the towering mountain peaks and trying to recall exactly what else Captain Umbrage had communicated to him before his departure.

Orion could make out the gist of the cryptic organizational structure of the rescue operation within the dense "FOG" (Foreign Operating Group) of acronyms that Captain Umbrage had hurled his way in rapid fire. Apparently there was a USSOCOM (United States Special Operations Command) operation integrated through JSOC (Joint Special Operations Command) that controlled the SMU (Special Mission Units), involving both LRSUs (Long Range Surveillance Units) and LRRPs (Long Range Reconnaissance Patrols), and that the ISA (Intelligence Support Activity) of this rescue operation was to be seriously supported by SAD (Special Activities Division) of the NCS (National Clandestine Services) of the CIA (Central Intelligence Agency) through a paramilitary SOG (Special Operations Group) of a government that would deny all knowledge of such an operation if the rescue mission was compromised in any way. Orion figured that all he really needed to remember was that the forces behind this particular acronymic operation were considered to be *special* and that the covert activities he was about to embark upon in the Himalayas was *highly classified.* All he really needed to know for the time being was that a Ranger-type RECONDO (Reconnaissance Commando) named Q. T. Bane was waiting for him high above Namche Bazaar at a place called Syangboche, located some 12,300 feet above sea level.

After passing above a hollow depression nearly atop a mountain and over a concentric cluster of small tile-roofed houses, which Orion assumed to be the village of Namche Bazaar, the chopper descended in a whirlwind of dust and stones, landing with its energy-attenuating skid gear upon a bleak dirt clearing that appeared more like an eagle's perch on the edge of a steep cliff than a plausible airstrip. When the turbine engine was turned off and the rotors gradually slowed to a stop, Orion stepped out into the rarefied air of a world above the clouds. He grabbed a pair of sunglasses from his pack and followed Segunda up a grassy slope and along a rough trail through wind-sculpted junipers to the entrance of an unlikely compound at the very top of the mountain.

Architecturally, the lodge was relatively simple: a series of rectangular gray block buildings composed of two stories with inclined roofs covered with green corrugated tin. Surrounding the compound was a stone wall that defined the extent of the leveled ground. In contrast to the humble Sherpa-style architecture was the natural setting—majestic, to say the least—and the physiological effect that such a panoramic spectacle can have on a first-time visitor is often profound. Overlooking deep green valleys and crystalline glaciers from impossible heights, while encompassed by even larger snow-covered immensities that loomed up and beyond from every direction, Orion was nearly overcome by an exhilarating feeling of astonishment, accompanied by a passing sensation of dizziness as he regained his breath and his bearings. He followed Segunda in silence through the gatehouse and into the courtyard of the compound with a strange and lingering impression of what he suddenly realized was, perhaps, his first perception of his own insignificance.

They were greeted by a man who looked very much like an American tourist—an average teahouse-trekking hippie with long strawberry-blond hair, a scruffy beard, and a faded Hard Rock T-shirt—with the exception that the shocking, badass scars on his well-muscled arms were much more frightening than any modern tribal tattoos, and he had an egregious attitude that virtually seeped out of every pore.

"You don't look like a seasoned operator to me," said the man, flashing what appeared to be a brief wink to Segunda. "Not Para! Not Gurkha! Not even Sherpa!" he barked in disgust. "Looks to me like another testosterone-soaked jock aimin' to get himself bagged and tagged for Queen and Country."

"I'm not English, I'm American," said Orion, removing his sunglasses and looking the man straight in the eye without flinching. "The name is Orion," he added. "And I assume you're Q. T. Bane."

"No shit, Sherlock. I know who you are … and I know who you're not!" said the man with the Hard Rock T-shirt and the badass scars, filling the narrow space between the disfigured warrior and the hero with a big brown glob of chewing tobacco juice. "I know that you're supposed to be some kind of hunter—on the hunt for your very own *living goddess*," he said with a sneer. "I also know that civvies like you don't know jack about the kind of wet work we're in for."

Refusing to be intimidated after coming so far, Orion hacked up some of his own saliva, added it to the terra firma, and said, "What you think about me is of no concern to me whatsoever. And you're right about my inexperience in military operations, but right now the only thing I have on my mind is the rescue of that so-called *living goddess* … and before it's too late!" Orion looked over to Segunda for some kind of support, but Segunda just smiled as if he were thoroughly enjoying the combative encounter.

"Time for you to wake up, hunter. Maybe you should stop thinking so much about rescue. Maybe it's time you started thinking about *revenge*," scoffed Bane.

"Why, you—" The mere thought of losing Joycelyn forever was more than Orion could stand, and in a swift and violent motion Orion surged forward, stepping inadvertently onto the toe of Bane's hiking boot as he shoved him hard. Bane fell backward to the ground, and before he could roll out of the way in a practiced maneuver, Orion was kneeling astride him, with his clenched fists hardened in furious anger. But before either man could make another move, the large curved blade of a Gurkha kukri knife flashed between them. It was Segunda, whose expression of delight had changed little with the intensity of the male bonding.

"You're not the kind of guy who would be in position like this at this time of day. But here you are and you cannot say that the terrain is entirely unfamiliar, although the air is thinner and the mountain mist is pretty hazy. You are at a remote mountain lodge and you are talking to a bleeding knucklehead. The lodge is either the Pilgrims Progress or the Heartbreak Hotel. All might become clear if you could just slip into the posture of an Indian yogi and begin to do some deep transcendental meditation. Then again, it might not. A small voice inside you insists that this epic lack of clarity is the result of too much sitting around already."

The sharp tenor of Segunda's monologue disarmed both Orion and Bane, as if two dim bulbs had suddenly been illuminated brightly within the mutual metropolis of their minds. They shook hands and moved on to a small group of picnic tables that constituted the outdoor restaurant of the remote and lofty lodge. A waiter joined them and asked if they would be having lunch. At first Bane declined, explaining that they had to move on to Pokhara ASAP to join up with a team of fast movers.

But Orion protested when he realized that he was so close to where Joycelyn was last seen. "Look, I'm sorry if we got off on the wrong foot … so to speak … but I've just got to see the place where she was living and teaching."

"Been there. Done that," replied Bane.

"I've got to see for myself where she was living," repeated Orion as he turned away, raising his sunglasses and squinting at the surrounding vistas with searching eyes.

"Seriously, dude, we already got all the recon we need from the locals. It's the same all over the district. The rubes swept through all the remote villages of the Sagarmatha, Janakpur, and Bagmati zones, and it looks like our first chance for an intercept is in the Annapurnas. That is, before they escape through the borders to the south, or worse, they might head through Mustang toward Dolpo and into the real wild west."

"Look, I get it," said Orion, fixing Bane with an imploring gaze. "We have to move fast … and I'm with you 100 percent. Really! I can assure you that I'm ready to do whatever needs to be done."

Bane only nodded.

"But you gotta give me a chance to see where she lived! Please, I need to see what it is she saw in this place … the school and the children she may have given her life for."

"Okay, Orion. You convinced me. It's only a few clicks beyond that ridge," Bane said, extending his bare, battle-scarred arm in the process. "And I reckon you'll have to acclimate some anyway to be of any use to me." Bane removed a pair of glacier glasses from a protective case and adjusted the leather side shields. "But I have to warn you," he said, "you won't find any children in that village."

Orion jumped up from his seat in anticipation. He turned slowly around and around in a staggering pirouette, marveling at the great snow-capped monstrosities surrounding him and trying to imagine how anyone could possibly find anyone else in the unmitigated vastness of this Solu-Khumbu wilderness.

"Leave your gear here, and make it fast," said Bane. "We have to depart this LZ (landing zone) well before sundown." Bane then called on a walkie-talkie for his unofficial sidekick, a Nepali Sherpa, to join them. "His name is Nyima Onchu Sherpa, but we like to call him Outré," said Bane when the man first appeared in the courtyard. The Sherpa wore casual Western-style clothing, but the grooves of his sunbaked face indicated a life spent in extreme high altitudes. The Sherpa Outré nodded to Bane and then to Segunda with obvious respect. "He isn't much good at conversation in English, but he knows these mountains and you can follow him to Khumjung while Segunda and I catch up on the latest scuttlebutt."

"What do you mean, follow him?" asked Orion.

"You'll see," said Bane. Both he and Segunda smiled knowingly. Outré was already heading out of the gateway toward the trail to the ridge. "Well, Segunda, it looks like you and me can grab us some lunch after all."

Orion retrieved a plastic water bottle from his expedition pack and started to run after the Sherpa, who was already approaching the crest of the ridge. It was then that he noticed that he was no longer in the Western Rockies, and that he was already nearly a mile higher up than his usual cross-country racing trails or even his routine ski patrol missions at Sun Valley. This was a place where the absence of oxygen rebuked the zealous as it chastened even the mightiest of desires. Running uphill in this altitude, Orion was immediately reminded of a song from the late seventies that equated love and oxygen in a direct metaphor: *too much, you soar too high; not enough, you're bound to die ...* he thought as he gasped, and he stopped running and eventually slowed to the rhythmic tempo of a fast-paced walk to the top of the ridge.

Following well behind Outré now, and descending along a narrow trail that wrapped around the flank of the holy mountain, Khumbila, Orion spotted a bevy of musk deer grazing peaceably among the high-altitude junipers and rhododendrons. The single trail soon widened into two parallel roads, allowing for directional travel to and from the village. He passed to the left of a Mani wall where Buddhist mantras were carved onto a series of flat stone tablets. Stone walls soon became a defining feature of the rustic causeways that led to the remote Sherpa village.

Nestled in a protected enclave of the mountain, Khumjung village appeared as a clean and orderly arrangement of rectangular block houses that were covered with either red or green tin roofs. Beyond the entrance gate, there were more Mani stones arrayed in a circular heap, followed by a long Mani wall dividing the two roadways that extended like a two-lane promenade into the heart of the village. The village was quiet; *Too quiet*, thought Orion as he made his way past the empty courtyards, past a whitewashed stupa and a pair of white-washed gompas with gilded spires. The gompas were encircled at their perimeter by a long line of prayer wheels that stood in solemnity and observance on their axes, each one silent and unmoving in the glare of the unblinking afternoon sun.

The village and its lofty setting were charming, to be sure, but there were far too few people in the streets, too few yaks and goats and porters to be seen. Orion was happy to find Outré, who appeared from a local bakery with a circular loaf of Tibetan-style bread, a large portion of which he shared politely with Orion. Still warm and fragrant from the oven, the lumpy bread had somehow been fried with butter and then baked to a variable consistency that ranged somewhere between doughy and crispy; the result was simple and satisfying as far as Orion was concerned, for he was beginning to appreciate the number of meals he had recently missed.

When Orion asked Outré about the location of the Sherpa schools that the children and their teachers were taken from, the Sherpa pointed vaguely in the direction of the empty courtyards. "Hillary," was all he said. And then the Sherpa walked down the street, back in the direction they had come, striding in a most determined manner.

Orion found himself running again, this time to the direction of the finger pointing and the empty courtyards. He came to a stone monument supporting a smiling bust of Sir Edmund Hillary, the founder of this and many other Sherpa schools. The smiling bust of Hillary, the Conqueror of Everest, sported a yellow prayer scarf that had been draped in veneration around the founder's neck. Beyond the monument were a line of single-story buildings with green corrugated tin roofs. The painted signs designating Khumjung Primary School and Khumjung Secondary School had been torn off the buildings and cast upon the ground. Orion raced from building to building, looking frantically for something—anything—that could prove that Joycelyn had not been harmed, something that could prove she had been there and had been happy, something that could prove to him that she still existed.

Orion darted around, and as he did so, he realized that his own footsteps were the only sounds to be heard. He stopped and listened, feeling the oppressive silence that pervaded the schoolyards and the classrooms close in around him. It was a deathly silence that reminded him of something he had almost succeeded in forgetting, something long ago that he wished had never happened, but once it had happened—once he had caused it to happen—and it was something that he sorely wished he could forget.

He had been ten years old, a boy in a lush green forest with a nondescript songbird and a brand-new BB gun. And Orion had been on the hunt. It so happened that he was hunting this nondescript songbird, singing high up in the trees, and although he could not see it clearly, he could hear its playful birdsong beckoning him, teasing him, frustrating him by calling attention to all of his ten-year-old shortcomings. He followed the songbird deeper and deeper into the forest as it lighted on one branch and then another. He aimed and fired his gun, which was so weakly sprung that he could actually see the BB arcing through the air and falling short of the mark.

Off again the songbird flew, deeper into the forest, taunting him, mocking him with a flourish of acoustic insults. Determined now, and with increasing fervor, Orion stalked this humiliating playmate from tree to tree, firing each time with renewed aim and greater precision, correcting each time for the failing trajectory. Every time he fired, the songbird vanished into the leaves of another tree, and Orion had to wait and wait—it seemed like forever—for the taunting, mocking, belittling little creature to reveal its new location by its increasingly contemptuous song. And then he saw the disparaging creature itself, perched casually on a high limb, looking down at him nonchalantly, as if it had dared to become so bold as if to feign innocence of its crime. Orion aimed, and with newfound cunning he anticipated the event, and then he fired ... and he watched the tiny ball as it floated upward along its course, arcing gracefully upward until it bowed and strived and ultimately reached the singing bird, which tumbled straight down dead to the ground with a final, discernable thump.

And then the world was silent. Silence like he'd never heard before. It was an appalling silence that spread within him like a cancer, destroying his composure and leaving him with the horror of a world that now existed without the sounds of either playfulness or laughter. Even the summer breezes that once calmed and cooled the fevered brow of the ten-year-old boy were hushed, and the entire stifled forest became as silent as a tomb. Holding the lifeless body of the silent songbird in his trembling hands, Orion was filled with the unbearable shame of his own humanity and the knowledge that he would never again hear the enticing innocence of such an unassuming voice. And although Orion, in his own maturity, would dedicate his best efforts to saving people and hunting things that were lost or injured, the sound of that deathly silence could never be forgotten—and it now loomed large.

Orion thrashed among the emptiness and disarray of the tiny classrooms and what appeared to be the makings of a small library, but now, with the benches and tables overturned and the books deranged like so many cobblestones on the dirt floor, he started to search the walls for papers and artwork that might have even her handwriting upon it. He stumbled into a newer block house with a single door off its hinges and two open windows. Inside, in what looked like a nunnery or a youth hostel, there was a line of five overturned beds and a small kitchen area that was devoid of any remaining cooking implements. On the walls there were still some shreds of photographs hanging from crude tacks and, straining to see in the limited light from an open window, Orion finally found what he was looking for. It was a photograph of Joycelyn surrounded by a class of beautiful, guileless children, and her face was beaming brightly, beaming with an obvious elation that shown like a jewel, beaming with the radiance of a true living goddess.

Orion stashed the photograph in his shirt pocket and headed out of the depleted dormitory, out into the vacant schoolyards, out along the forsaken promenade, out through the unattended gatehouse and out of the empty village with a fierce and increasing urgency. In the distance, Orion could see that darkening shadows were forming on the contours of the surrounding snow-covered peaks. What had once been towering giants, glistening snowy-white and pristine, were now turning slowly with the relentless passage of the day to more sinister and alarming shades of dusk, which—along with the oppressive perception of the surrounding silence—reminded Orion that *time is always of the essence.*

Orion could see, far-off, the three characteristic peaks of Ama Dablam surging up into the skyline. *"Ama Dablam,"* thought Orion, *"the great mother, or ama, protecting her two precious children,"* which stood on either side of the pyramidal massif. Every aspiring mountaineer knew the shape and thrust of this adamantine and visually dramatic formation. It was a symbol of the benevolence of the natural world for the Sherpa people. However, on this particular day, with the deathly silence of the tomb on his mind, and the perception of nightfall now creeping upon him, and the acute awareness that his time remaining to find Joycelyn alive was running out, all that Orion could see before him was a relentless foreshadowing that the mother and her missing children were all too rapidly disappearing into the dark.

5. Pleiades: A Lost Generation of Doves

The staccato whirl of the helicopter blades chopping violently through the vortices of their own turbulent wake served as an acoustic emissary for the howling state of emergency that now existed—physically representing, in so many painful decibels, the continuous pressure of unmitigated urgency that drove Orion forward. On any other occasion, the concordance of such propulsive impulses—given the demanding situation at hand—might have acted as a mental hypnotic that would gradually attenuate the strained attentiveness of the hunter, lulling him into a brief respite of blissful shut-eye within the constant assurances of the comforting drone. On any other rescue mission, he might even surrender to a brief moment or two of sleep and allow the machinery to go on its course without his constant state of awareness. But not this occasion, not this mission, not this particular evening. Orion was bright-eyed and wide awake as the helicopter beat its boisterous way westward across the central region of the Himalayan foothills, and he was ready to go as soon as it settled down on its skids at the outskirts of Pokhara.

Located in the lap of the Annapurna Himal, Pokhara was once an important trading place on the routes from Kathmandu to Jumla in the west, and from India to Tibet, which lay beyond the majestic mountain peaks to the north. The sun was setting low in the sky when Orion and his paramilitary cohorts, Bane and Segunda, and the accompanying Sherpa, Outré, exited the chopper with their gear and stepped blindly into the exhaust-filled swirl of the turbines, each man bending low to avoid the sweep of the rotors with their overarching scythes. They were immediately approached by a 4WD Toyota Land Cruiser that drove right up to the cusp of the landing zone. On top of the truck was a rack of spotlights and a rooftop cargo basket that was partially filled with bundles of gear. Inside were two shadowy men. The driver leaned out of his window.

"Hop in, ladies!" shouted the driver, a well-built man with short-cropped hair, whose service with a smile reflected more than a modicum of contempt. "Time to dance with the devil himself … Time to insert one FNG—freaking new guy," he added, grinning and pointing a thumb in Orion's direction—"into our designated area of operation."

They loaded their gear onto the roof rack of the Land Cruiser, and Orion secured the load under a cargo net by extending the hooks of the flat bungee cords farther forward. Then the men crammed into two sets of bench seats behind the driver and his passenger, who did not bother to turn around. The Land Cruiser surged forward, and the JBL sound system began to emit the driving beat of Eminem's *Lose Yourself,* blaring at decibels nearly approaching those of the helicopter: *"One shot … one opportunity … one moment."* Orion couldn't help but think that every word, every directive, every driving thread of the beat was addressed directly to him … and then he noticed that every hardheaded hombre in the speeding SUV was rocking and nodding in unison to the same determinative beat.

They drove westward in the direction of the sunset and into the twilight along the Pokhara-Baglung-Beni road, along a stretch of rocks and loose dirt that would have been brutal to trek. It was raining hard, and the Land Cruiser had to churn over standing water and landslides that tilted the vehicle to extreme angles. When it grew dark, they drove more slowly, watchfully, using the spotlights to illuminate the roadway. Then things got scary—the brace of spotlights tipped toward vertical, and the truck began to slide sideways in the mud.

The driver turned off the music and eased the Land Cruiser carefully around the edge of the landslide, dangerously close to what might have been a steep drop into Never-Never Land. Breathing was easier at this moderate altitude, and Orion breathed a noticeable sigh of relief when the vehicle surmounted the slippery mound and returned to level ground.

The driver peered into the rearview mirror at the faces of the men in the back as if he were looking for something—telltale signs of fear, perhaps. "Bane? Is that you, Bane?"

"Roger that," replied Sergeant Bane.

"Must be a small world after all," said the driver.

"Somebody has to keep you lunatics in check," added Bane. "After what happened the last time out, I'm surprised you condors are still in business."

"Look here, first shirt, it's all in the handbook, in case you hadn't noticed."

"What are you talking about, LaFleche?"

"*De opresso liber*, recondo man. *De opresso liber.* You give liberties, and we take liberties—it's as simple as that! It's a perfect circle."

"*Lunatics,* like I said," replied Bane.

"*Small world for the taking,* like I said," echoed LaFleche.

They drove for what seemed like hours, stopping occasionally to check out a large obstacle on the road or to a secure a path around a dangerous rockslide. The jeep track became increasingly narrow beyond the village of Beni and was littered with rocks and deep, water-filled potholes, and it often approached sheer cliffs and blind turns that left little room to spare. The rain had slowed to a misty drizzle when they finally arrived at a place called Tatopani, literally "hot water," where Bane instructed Outré and Segunda to check everyone in for the night. Then Orion followed Bane and the two shadowy men down a series of stone steps along the riverside to a steaming pool of hot mineral springs, which, after carefully removing their hiking boots, they entered fully clothed. The area around the pool was lit by torches that wavered with the breeze and cast a meager light upon the steamy, shadowy scene. Within a few feet of the rectangular pool, the river was running fast with rainwater, and they had to speak loudly to be heard above the din.

Orion could see that the man named LaFleche was tall and well-muscled with hair that had been shaved down to nubs. The other shadowy man was smaller and appeared to be younger than Bane and LaFleche. "LaFleche …?" said Orion, by way of introduction. "Is that French Canadian Commando or French Foreign Legion?"

"Neither," said LaFleche with an unsettling grin. "None of the above," he added. "You gotta think global, newbie. We're corporate, and proud of it." As he spoke, he began to undress, wringing out each item of clothing hard and placing it on the ground beside him outside of the pool. "We create our own land of opportunity in whatever country happens to provide the appropriate means and financial incentives."

"What you guys are is disgusting," said Sergeant Bane, sounding somewhat less than convincing and yet following suit in the manner of undressing and wringing out.

"You mean you have your own private army?" asked Orion incredulously.

"Don't be ridiculous," said Sergeant Bane, "these hoodlums are contracted to perform specific operations in coordination with higher authorities—which in this turkey shoot happens to be me."

"Ah, he's just mad because he has to take orders, while we have the ability to tell enlisted military personnel to pound sand—or snow, as the case may be—and we do so at every opportunity."

"So I take it you guys are some kind of mercenaries?" said Orion.

"Now you're getting nasty," said LaFleche with a sneer, "and we only just met. This talkative fellow's name is Dahmer, by the way … and you can call me LaFleche."

"Yo," said Dahmer, who had been conspicuously silent up to that point. He flashed a youthful, almost impish smile that settled into a confident grin that seemed more fitting with his finely chiseled muscularity.

"I'm glad to meet you guys. My name is Orion."

"Now there's a name you don't hear every day," said LaFleche. "Is that some kind of stage name? I mean, are you some kind of actor?"

"No, it's my real name."

"Cuz this here mission is no Star Trek episode, newbie. There's nobody gonna beam your ass out of this neck of the woods when things get to being dangerous."

"I'm ready to do whatever needs to be done, and to help out in any way I can."

"Nice highfalutin words, *Orion*, but from my particular point of view you've got nothing to offer. We might as well call you 'Junkless.'"

Orion just shook his head in amusement and wrung the water out of his shirt. "Yeah, well, sometimes Junkless can be a real cool hand."

At this point, Bane stepped in, so to speak. "What he *does* have is priority, and he also has deniability. What you morons bring to the table is plausibility and fear-factor."

"*Plausible deniability*, you say—now where have I heard that before?" chuckled LaFleche.

"It's in the contractor's field manual," said Dahmer.

"You see, Orion," explained Bane. "This mission has humongous priority for HQ. If it were just a simple disappearance, there would be no ruckus. People are *disappeared* all the time in this part of the world. But the kidnapping of an American *beauty queen* ... now that's some serious consternation." As he spoke, Bane pushed himself up from the hot springs to a sitting position at the side of the pool, with his feet still dangling in the water. "It's like they went and kidnapped the president's daughters or something. It's like they shoved their grubby fingers under the dress of the Statue of Liberty herself—or would that be a toga?"

"You would be referring to her stola," said Segunda, who appeared with a pile of towels. "The bad guys you are referring to would be shoving their grubby fingers under Statue of Liberty's stola."

"So what's the word, first shirt?" queried LaFleche, referring to the marching orders from HQ.

"SSDD—same situation, different day—only this time you keep your pickle in your pants and try not to lay waste to everything and everyone around you."

"Wrong answer, Bane," barked LaFleche. "You cut us some slack or we're out of here as soon as Bob arrives."

"Who's Bob?" asked Orion.

"Stands for Big Orange Ball, doofus," Dahmer chimed in with a smile.

"All right, same situation, new day," Bane acquiesced. "We go deep reconnaissance downrange, with passive intelligence from the rear echelons. This here sweep through the schoolyards has gotten way out of hand, and it's far too well-coordinated. We aim for you to break their concentration by any and all means, and I am authorized to permit you to take direct action whenever practicable. Is that enough slack for you, LaFleche?"

"That's what I needed to hear, top kick," said LaFleche while gaining an affirmative nod from Dahmer. "Consider us involved!"

"That's good, right?" asked Orion. "What are we going to do now?"

"We're gonna sleep on it, rookie," said LaFleche, pushing himself up and out of the hot springs. "Bob'll get here soon enough."

Walking up the ancient steps of the torch-lit spa in single file, with towels wrapped around their waists and carrying their wet clothes in front of them in silence, the troupe looked very much like a medieval abomination of monks.

At daybreak, the unit breakfasted together, and then they piled into the Land Cruiser and headed north into the Annapurna Himal. The road was still slick and muddy from the previous day's rains, and the air was infused with the mossy aromas of lush green forests. The clouds that had been obscuring the distant mountains when they first started out were inspired by Bob to dissipate or to sink into the deep valleys, revealing the spectacular Dhaulagiri massif that spread out wide to the left; to the right the distinctive "fishtail peak" of Machhapuchhare surged skyward among the uppermost pinnacles of the Annapurnas.

Following the bends of the Kali Gandaki River, the SUV ascended steeply toward the village of Ghasa, climbing out of the valleys and along the deepest gorge that Orion had ever seen. The vegetation changed rapidly from almost tropical to pine and coniferous forests, and the air grew noticeably thinner. On the road there were trains of overburdened donkeys and small herds of black-faced sheep; in the air there were vultures and other birds of prey gliding on the thermals and occasionally sweeping low overhead as if to check out the unlikely tourists. The men of the long range reconnaissance patrol made a brief pit stop at a local teahouse, where they sipped ginger tea at the base of a waterfall, and then they headed onward as far on the rock-strewn road that the rugged Land Cruiser could manage. When they could no longer drive, LaFleche locked up the bulk of their nonessential gear in the truck, and they headed out on foot into the forbidden kingdom of Mustang.

The pace was fast, and Orion liked it that way. At first, he was able to keep up with Segunda and Outré; at first, his athletic conditioning paid off; at first, he thought he had everything he needed to be successful. But then, there is something to be said about acclimatization to such rarified air, and after two hours of steady climbing, he slipped back among the trailing members of the deep reconnaissance patrol.

"Hey, Dahmer," said Orion. "Is that your last name or a nickname?"

"It's just a name they gave me, dude."

"Tell him how you got your nickname, Dahmer," shouted LaFleche.

"It's no big secret," he replied.

"Go on, tell him," nagged LaFleche.

"Look, I'm not ashamed of it. I like rugby, and it was just a bumper sticker."

"You got your nickname from a bumper sticker?" quipped Orion in surprise.

"It's not what goes into a man that defiles him," said LaFleche. It's—"

"It's what he puts on the bumper of his jeep," Sergeant Bane blurted out, obviously getting the gist of the humor.

"What *exactly* did it say about rugby players on your bumper sticker?" asked Orion.

"Forget it … it was just a bumper sticker. I don't see it as a big deal."

"Okay, Dahmer … whatever you say," said Orion.

They hiked through the Thakali village of Ghasa, with its flat-roofed houses and accoutrements of Tibetan Buddhism, and they trudged up a steep incline to Kalopani, where they crossed a narrow suspension bridge and headed higher up on increasingly precipitous paths. They trudged over the gravel road, passing mule trains and locals carrying impressive loads of firewood.

After several more hours of trekking, they were greeted by the duly appointed representatives of the Communist Party of Nepal, a.k.a. Maoists, who demanded a tariff from Segunda and Outré as a contribution to their cause. The situation was quickly explained to the lagging party, who were now subject to the same demand. Apparently shaking down tourists was SOP, or standard operating procedure, for those engaged in the ongoing "People's War." Judging from the antique carbines that were currently being pointed in the direction of the intruders to the forbidden kingdom, it looked like the aforementioned donations were considered to be mandatory.

There were half a dozen Maoists with half that many carbines. They were young and yet looked pretty fierce in their camouflage uniforms as far as Orion was concerned. But they also looked nervous when they saw the general size and excessive muscularity of these particular tourists. In an uncharacteristic gesture of cordiality, Bane instructed Segunda to pay the young men the going rate for ingress into the Mustang region for the purposes of trekking beyond the Annapurna circuit, which he did. The Maoists even provided the party with a receipt to serve as a colorful souvenir. LaFleche was so pleased with the amicable transaction that he instructed Dahmer to take a "reconnaissance" photograph of these fine young Maoists, along with their archaic armament.

Orion was about to join the group portrait when LaFleche waved him away. Dahmer pulled a 35mm camera with telephoto lens out of his pack and held it out to frame the picture. As the Maoists moved together and smiled proudly for the photograph, Orion noticed something curious: for rather than focusing the camera for a clear shot, Dahmer appeared to be bracing the camera against some kind of impact.

Before anyone could react, there was an explosion of sound, and three of the Maoists fell backward to the ground. The unexpected detonation of the shotgun shell, taken together with the fall of their comrades in arms, was too much for the flanks, who dropped their guns and started running in all directions. Taking up one of the carbines, Dahmer checked its load and then, shouldering the weapon, picked off two of the fleeing Maoists in rapid succession, calmly, coolly, like a highly trained sniper.

Orion watched in horror as Segunda stepped over one of the three Maoists who were writhing on the ground. The body stiffened and then completely relaxed, and as Segunda quickly stepped over to the next wounded man, Orion could see clearly that the first man's throat had been cut ... and then another ... and then another. And then Segunda turned and faced Orion with the bloody knife and a glaring strain of smile he had never seen before in his life.

"I know what you're thinking," said Segunda to Orion. "Are there six dead Maoists or only five? Well, to tell you the truth, in all the excitement, I've kinda lost track myself. But being that this here is the sharp edge of a forty-four-meter drop, along the deepest gorge in all the world, and that bloke ran clean off that cliff, you've to ask yourself one question: 'Was that Maoist lucky?' ... Well, was he ... dude?"

As though they were responding to Segunda's rhetorical question, the men of the deep reconnaissance patrol moved to the extreme verge of the precipitous cliff and, with both curiosity and caution, they peered over the edge.

With no Maoists left alive to interrogate, Sergeant Bane was not entirely pleased with the outcome of the engagement, and he let Dahmer and LaFleche know it. The situation was apparently smoothed over when LaFleche assured Bane that they had already done their homework and that there were a lot more Maoists where the others came from, stating, "There is a whole nest of the freaking commies camped out in the apple orchards up near the village of Marpha."

At the time, Orion was more interested in what Segunda was doing to the dead bodies. In quick succession, Segunda had applied the slashing edge of his Gurkha kukri knife to each side of the dead Maoists heads, promptly lopping off the ears of each accessible dead man. Then Segunda reached into his pack, pulled out a spotted bolt of crude fabric, and meticulously unrolled the handwoven cloth on the ground like a sacred scroll. One side of the swath of cloth was clean and unblemished, and on the other side there were matched pairs of macabre trophies. Orion stood in astonishment as Segunda carefully placed the ten freshly harvested human ears onto the clean cloth surface and slowly rolled the lumpy scroll to a close.

"What in heaven's name is he doing?" asked Orion.

Bane, who was scribbling some numbers into a small notebook, replied by saying, "Everybody keeps tabs in his own way."

"Is it some form of symbolic punishment?" continued Orion. "Did they fail to listen to reason while they were alive, or some such thing?"

"Negative, Orion. It's more terrifying than that to the locals … it's so they won't be able to *hear* anything in the current state they're in."

Segunda nodded in affirmation as he placed the gruesome scroll back into his pack.

"Come on. They're dead as doornails," said Orion to Segunda, who was smiling with obvious contentment. "They can't hear anything you say with or without ears."

"You Westerners certainly have a lot to learn about the *intermediate state*," said Segunda as he cleaned the curved cutting edge and gingerly sheathed the kukri knife.

Before Orion could pursue the question further, the lead parties of the long range reconnaissance patrol moved out, trekking steadily up the trail into grassy meadows and higher through a series of alpine woods. Crossing several times over the Kali Gandaki River on narrow suspension bridges, they trekked to a point where the river rose up to meet them, and they continued hiking beside the river bed, climbing higher and higher into increasingly barren terrain. They passed small villages that appeared to have been abandoned and small plots of unattended mustard crops nestled within patches of unlikely farmland, all set among the towering peaks of Dhaulagiri and Annapurna. A strong wind was blowing up from the south through the river valley as they climbed, and it seemed to have cleared a path through the clouds, which were strewn in thin layers on either side of the pass up ahead.

The trail flattened out upon a desert-like terrain, and the long range reconnaissance patrol stopped at what appeared to be an abandoned police station. LaFleche informed Bane with hand signals that the so-called "nest" of Maoists was located up ahead, and that due caution and silence was called for. Dahmer sat down next to Orion and dug into his expedition pack. He produced four black cylinders, which he handed over to Orion and whispered, "You can throw, can't ya?"

Orion nodded. He read the words "STUN GRENADE" in white letters on the side of each canister and he nodded once again.

"They're just *flashbangs*, rookie ... totally nonlethal. Just pull and chuck 'em when and where it counts," continued Dahmer, who had armed himself with a Heckler & Koch Mark-23 pistol.

Orion noticed that both Bane and LaFleche were brandishing similar weapons, which Bane explained were OHWS (offensive handgun weapon systems), comprised of a .45 caliber pistol, a laser aiming module, and a sound-and-flash suppressor. They moved out, concealing the OHWS weaponry in their clothes, and proceeded to trek onward like any other group of tourists. Only, this group of tourists had serious badass intentions.

It was getting late in the day and shadows were lengthening when they passed by the ancient Thakali village of Tukuche, which looked deserted, and then they came upon the Maoist encampment near the village of Marpha. What was once a Tibetan refugee settlement, and then a horticulture research station, was now an indoctrination center for the Maoists who had taken over the area. From his vantage point, Orion could see that there were about a dozen male and female children, ranging from about ten to fifteen years old, who were visible in the cantonments, presumably undergoing indoctrination in the study of political labels drenched in hatred and the appropriate categorizations of *oppressor* and *oppressed.* Several older Maoists, dressed in traditional camouflage pants and sneakers, were busy making an example of a reluctant recruit by beating him senseless with a wooden stick before wrapping him up in a jute bag. There was a band of skinny teenage militia looking on as security in front of one of the expropriated houses; others were holding down an unfortunate villager, who must have found fault with their overly convincing methods of instruction.

Orion searched the foregrounds of the village for signs of Joycelyn, hoping beyond hope that this would be the end of his journey—hoping that his paramilitary colleagues would be able to rescue Joycelyn and her kidnapped schoolchildren in one swift operation, hoping that he would be sharing his two-man tent with the love of his life that very night. As he searched the foreground of the village to no avail, Orion spotted two teenage communists wearing camouflage headbands and holding vintage 0.303 caliber bolt-action Enfield rifles on their shoulders. He noticed that both of them were wearing T-shirts: one was sporting the image of Britney Spears, and the other an image of David Beckham. He decided that these fashionable bad guys would make a suitable target for a flashbang.

Approaching the camp from the cover of a continuous stone wall and around a pen of bleating yearling goats, the long range reconnaissance patrol was nearly upon the nest of Maoists by the time they were noticed. Bane gave the signal, and all hell broke loose when a swarm of stun grenades detonated in every sector of the encampment. In a matter of minutes, each of the gun-wielding Maoists was summarily dispatched, along with a number of elder statesmen who came running out of the house. Sergeant Bane killed two bad guys according to military SOP, with two shots to the chest and one to the head, leaving the tangos nice and quiet and dead. LaFleche used an abbreviated double-tap method to bag his quarries, while Dahmer took home the prize with his patented one-shot-one-kill approach to the problem.

Segunda herded the young recruits up against a stone wall by brandishing his fearsome kukri knife, and with the help of Outré, who had not participated directly in the melee, he began to question the schoolchildren, many of whom were crying. Segunda related the gist of the translation to the others secondhand, in his characteristic manner of speaking. It turned out that most of these children had indeed been kidnapped from the Khumbu or Everest region, but that they had been split up for some reason and loaded onto different buses.

"It's just some clueless young men and ugly girls," said Bane to LaFleche.

"Copy that," said LaFleche. "Not one of them likely to be playing queen for a day in the brothels of Delhi or Mumbai. Apparently they just arrived, so it's unlikely that we'll have any better luck further up in Mustang."

"What does that mean?" asked Orion, still trembling from the sounds and sights of the direct action.

"It means that we hightail it out of here to the nearest LZ, which is just a few clicks up the road at Jomsom," answered LaFleche.

On the ground, Segunda was relieving the dead Maoists of their ears, as before. Overhead, a colony of vultures was already gathering for a feast.

"Don't worry, Orion," said Bane, who was taking notes. "We've got all the escape routes down below covered, and there is no way they are getting your gal and her kiddies across the border to India by bus anytime soon."

Sergeant Bane and Outré prepared to march the rescued children back to the parked Land Cruiser—where they would evacuate them directly to a safe house in Pokhara—before rejoining the operation again in the remote environs of Dolpo. With the exception of those striking battle scars, which were still visible at the level of his rolled-up sleeves, Sergeant Q. T. Bane, with his scruffy beard and long, blond hair held in place with a woven headband, still looked every bit like a Nepal teahouse trekker from times gone by.

LaFleche moved in close and reminded Bane to make sure to bring their "power tools," which were locked up in the truck.

Orion looked around at the carnage and the children. "There are twelve schoolchildren here, if I counted correctly," he said, "including the boy we cut out of the bag. How are you going to fit them all in just the one Land Cruiser?"

"That's what the roof racks are for," said Sergeant Bane. And then, shouldering his expedition pack, he started back down the road the same way they had come. Without turning, Bane raised his hand in a gesture of farewell to the remaining members of the deep reconnaissance patrol, and one small fraction of an entire generation of lost doves followed safely in his footsteps toward home.

6. Peaceful and Wrathful Emanations

The wind was at their backs when the four men of the deep reconnaissance patrol continued their quest, and it increased gradually in intensity amidst a golden sunset. Then a strange grayness came slowly upon them, like autumn twilight, reflecting neither day nor night. The towering mountains looked down on every step. Orion noticed that the scenery had changed from a landscape of verdant alpine meadows and shrubs to a surrealistic high-desert terrain where the river slowed, becoming wider and flatter as it worked its way through the barren, windswept hills. They climbed steadily along the valley floor to the riverside village of Jomsom.

The sounds of jingling bells signaled the approach of Mustang ponies and a small drove of goats that were being guided to lower pastures by women wearing aprons made on hand looms and yak-hair scarves wrapped around their waists. The women passed quickly without so much as noticing the men, as though they were simply tourists or traders on the ancient salt trade route between the northern plains of India and Tibet. Segunda went on ahead to reconnoiter and to secure food and lodging for the night.

The men crossed over the Kali Gandaki on an old wooden bridge. They passed by the looted remains of the district hospital, with all its glass windows shattered, and by the burned-out remnants of what appeared to have been a Royal Nepal Army camp. They checked out a communications building, which was devoid of wireless equipment and electricity but still supported a large antenna in plain view. LaFleche sent Orion and Dahmer along to find Segunda while he attempted to contact HQ with a portable squad radio he had packed in. The remainder of the village looked largely untouched by the recent destruction, with firewood stacked neatly in rows on the flat roofs of the quaint whitewashed houses. Everywhere Orion looked, there were tall poles brandishing multicolored Tibetan prayer flags that were flapping wildly in the wind.

Segunda was waiting for them in the center of the deserted, stone-paved street. He directed Orion and Dahmer to a teahouse lodge within the main village, instructing them in his usual second-person perspective, "Eat and sleep well tonight, for tomorrow you may die." Then he left again, to keep watch and to direct LaFleche to the guesthouse.

Inside the lamp-lit dining room, the air was filled with the mouthwatering aromas of Thakali home cooking, the simmering broths of lamb and chicken stews fusing faintly with the heady smells of sweet spices and the biting piquancy of fermented mustard greens. They were served by an old woman with a round face and high cheekbones who brought out an appetizer of sukuti sadeko, a homemade lamb jerky, followed by a steaming chicken-gizzard sauté. Orion and Dahmer savored the apple brandy that was served to the table and, while they were waiting for LaFleche to join them, ordered a random series of main courses by pointing to an unintelligible menu without actually speaking, and without much consideration for the culinary particulars at hand.

The meal was served on stainless-steel trays, each containing a large mountain of rice or buckwheat starch along with lesser amounts of yak, lamb, or chicken parts which were surrounded by a series of smaller dishes of pickled vegetables, spiced tomato chutney, stewed mustard greens, potato curry, marinated brown beans, and sour yogurt smeared with white radish paste.

LaFleche arrived and joined them at the table, announcing that he had finally been able to contact Captain Q. T. Umbrage and to get an update of current events.

"How is Grudge doing?" asked Orion, bursting with newfound familiarity.

"He's back in Kathmandu," said LaFleche. "They had to move into dicey new digs after the palace massacre, considering that they were situated a bit too close for comfort and discretion."

"Yeah, like right across the street," said Dahmer.

"I mean, how is Grudge doing on this particular mission?" repeated Orion.

"That's what I was saying, newbie—the new HQ in Kathmandu is only temporary, and the field communications still leave something to be desired. It appears that the military have all the major roads blocked to India, and they are monitoring traffic at the borders twenty-four-seven. Looks like some part of a bus caravan made a run for the border at Nepalgunj while we were up here scouting around Mustang."

Orion, feeling a sudden tingling sensation of pins and needles, swept his hair back with his fingers and leaned forward on his forearms.

LaFleche polished off a tumbler of apple brandy and continued. "Some of the schoolgirls on those buses were from the Solu-Khumbu region … but no teachers and no beauty queen … so the current best guess is that the main group fled north through Jajarkot, or possibly through Tulsipur to Rolpa and Rukum, where the Maoists have a stronghold and the government forces have all bailed out."

"That sounds really bad, doesn't it? It's bad, right?" asked Orion with an intense curiosity bordering on panic. His latest mouthful of toasted beans, immersed in a fragrant dressing of pure mustard oil, created a distinctive burning sensation as it slid slowly down his throat.

"No!" said LaFleche. "What's bad for the royal military is often good for us." He spoke with an indecorous exhibition of teeth. "It's only when the royally appointed ones fail to deliver, with all their practiced military precision and their snooty ranks and their predictable behaviors—it's only when *all the king's men* have undeniably failed to deliver a tinker's damn worth of corrective action … when it appears that the whole blasted country is going to hell in a handbasket … when every cleancut, spit 'n' polish, by-the-book pretender to the kingdom of glory has come and turned tail or gone belly-up and the entire mission is grievously at risk, without a single, solitary shred of substance accomplished—that's when the powers-that-be begin to appreciate guys like me and Dahmer here. We are one enterprise that never fails to deliver, 'cuz we are driven by both the best and the worst of all human motivations ….."

Without specifying the exact nature of these particular motivations, or even hinting at what—in his way of thinking—the best and the worst of all human motivations might actually be, LaFleche theatrically cracked his neck sideways and continued on his course. "Sometimes I get to thinking that we are the only ones alive who manage to keep our eyes on the prize ….." As LaFleche spoke, both he and Dahmer appeared to drift off into the lost horizons of some far-distant reveries, as if they were each in search of something that was both mysterious and strangely ineffable.

Orion interrupted the philosophical contemplations with an abrupt and direct question: "How can you expect to accomplish what the local police, the national army, and the secretive services cannot?"

"We expect to accomplish our goals because we do not let operational difficulties interfere with our strategic plan of action. We are not bounded by orders; we are not bounded by permissions; we are not bounded by officially approved procedures. You might say that we are unbridled by any and all constraints."

Dahmer simply nodded in agreement.

"And what, may I ask, *is* our strategic plan of action?" asked Orion.

"Our strategic plan is to *Seek* … and to *Strike* … and to *Kill* the infernal bastards who are currently manhandling your girl!" said LaFleche, the latter phrase issuing emphatically through nearly clenched teeth. "And then we mean to collect our just rewards," he added.

"How can I thank you," asked Orion, "and more importantly, how can I help you?"

"You've already helped us by carrying the torch, Orion. You see, this manhunt—I mean, this extrajudicial assassination—has been given high priority by top brass and by royal decree. These have got to be the big dogs who concocted this scheme, and that makes them an extremely high-value target. You see, Orion, the terrorists who took your *beauty queen* obviously knew exactly what they were doing. They are cutting the heart out of one country—that being the innocence of the USA—while they are taking the soul out of yet another, that being the peaceful kingdom of Nepal."

"Really, you guys," said Orion, biting down hard and then releasing his lower lip. "What do you need right now to be successful, and how in the world can I help?"

"You, hunter, provide the aim, while we provide the equal and opposite force!" And that was the last thing LaFleche said that night, but he said it with such conviction as to almost be convincing.

A few minutes later another meal appeared, one of giant dumplings and dal bhat, a lentil stew with steamed rice, curried potatoes and peas, and a spicy-sour relish of rhubarb and tomatoes that was served on a plate with small molds pressed in it, such that every item in the meal was separated and could be mixed as one liked. LaFleche signaled for Orion to bring the plate to Segunda, who was found seated on the ground, on lookout, just outside the guesthouse.

The wind was blowing hard in low shrieks when Orion approached Segunda, who was sitting motionless, sheltered from the cold blasts by a poncho that was supported in part by the firmament of an old stone wall. Orion stopped and listened against the wind; he could hear that Segunda was praying—to himself, it seemed—in perfect accordance with his thoroughly second-person persona.

"At this time, the fierce, turbulent, utterly unbearable hurricane of past actions will be swirling around you, driving you on," said Segunda, speaking with his eyes closed. "Do not be afraid! This is your bewildered perception. You imagine that you are being pursued by terrifying wild animals, by carnivorous ogres, by hordes of negative beings, and that you are struggling through snow, through rain, through blizzards and darkness. You will hear the sounds of mountains crumbling, of lakes flooding, of fires spreading, and the roar of fierce winds. Terrified, you will try to flee, but your path will be cut off by three frightening precipices, and you will feel as though you are on the verge of falling. Do not be afraid! These are not truly precipices; they are points of aversion, attachment, and delusion. You must save yourself from falling into even lower existences. Do not forget this!"

Hearing these strange words, Orion thought it best to leave the steaming tray of food for Segunda without disturbing him. And then Orion returned to the shelter of the guesthouse and the oblivion of dreamless sleep.

The next day, the sky was overcast with a layer of high clouds, and the air was crisp and cool. A giant twin-engine Mi-8MT, a.k.a. "Hip-H," helicopter landed on its wheels at what passed for an airport in Jomsom, and they were soon beating their way westward around the glistening shoulder of the Dhaulagiri massif in the direction of the high, lonesome plateaus of Dolpo. Orion and Segunda were sitting together on fold-down seats directly across from Dahmer and LaFleche in the cavernous cargo bay of the transport chopper. LaFleche was chewing tobacco. Peering out behind him through a circular porthole window, Orion could see that they were following the meandering course of a high river valley, flying fast and close to the ground. He espied an elongated village stretched thinly on the banks of the shallow river; there were clusters of closely spaced houses and what appeared to be barley fields terraced into the rocky slopes of a decidedly inhospitable environment. There were no discernable roads.

When Orion inquired where they were heading, in reference to where they might be landing, LaFleche informed him, "That village you see down there would be Dunai!" he shouted. "It was supposed to be the district headquarters … but we won't be landing there!"

"Why not?" shouted Orion.

"No! You don't want to go there!" affirmed Segunda.

"Because the communist guerillas killed about thirty policemen there last week!" barked LaFleche, "and I expect that we might get the same kind of reception!"

It was not a comforting thought to have in mind when they landed in Juphal, a mere handful of kilometers farther west. Nor was it a comforting sight to see the giant helicopter rise up and away in a cloud of dust and fog as it beat a hasty retreat.

They moved fast in a westward direction into the forbidding land of Dolpo, following the winding course of the river on narrow trails cut into the rocky hillsides by ageless and enduring caravans. After a few hours, they came upon a number of unattended rice fields terraced into the mountain. They crossed over the river single file on a flimsy suspension bridge and continued on to the west, passing quietly beneath a cluster of crude houses that stood out on promontories overlooking the river valley. Orion could see that the houses had wooden windows, which were tightly shuttered; some of the houses had carved wooden faces mounted high on the roofs, and others had constructed effigies that peered out menacingly at the uninvited guests. They trekked along the river with due caution, for they had entered a land that was guarded by primeval spirits which were apparently still active, being summoned or abated by ancient practices that predated the arrival of the more contemplative religions.

Orion felt an uncomfortable chill when they passed in view of an old hilltop fortress—or possibly it was a primitive temple of sorts—which appeared to be guarding the approach to the river valley, its commanding buttresses manned by no one alive, yet the long-faded tendrils of four flag-like streamers wafted like so many animated serpents swimming in the breeze.

Beyond the fortress, the river valley widened and the trail continued upward through an area of loose rocks into a barren, waterless terrain of naked earth thinly covered in fine layers of brown and yellow and gray dust. They trekked hard and fast and on into the latter part of the day, spreading out in space and time until they were far apart in terms of linear formation. Orion could not see the man in front or behind him, yet he knew that they were there, united in purpose, bound by a common sense of mission into a cohesive troop of hominids that pushed on with a primal determination that resided somewhere between ape and essence. There would be no cute and cuddly snow leopards to search for, as in the 139th Hardy Boys mystery; nor would any of the figurative felines be looking benevolently down upon them in accordance with the distorted ruminations of new-ageist tyro-monks; nor would this troop be likely to give up and go home anytime soon without actually finding what they were looking for. This was a troop of altogether hard men who were becoming harder with each forsaken step. They were becoming hard in the manner of Nietzsche's diamond—the kind of *hard* that is needed to impress one's superlative will upon the world, upon the millennia; the kind of *hard* that is needed to bend and break the will of all resistance, of all opposition; the kind of *hard* that is needed to write history.

Ascending more steeply now through a large expanse of meadows populated by a herd of black wooly yaks that were grazing on the grassy slopes, they continued on past sundown and into the gloaming time, climbing higher and higher up a rocky slope that ran through a forest of evergreens, and then beyond that forest into a zone of transition where all such vegetation ceased, emerging beyond the merest sense of awe or fear into an abiding, concentrated state of mind that is naturally cultivated above the timberline. Above the timberline, Orion knew that one does not have the luxury of remaining on a distracted path.

They traveled far out on the upper flank of the mountain, traversing upon a ribbon of dust that seemed to go on for miles without an apparent end and without a landmark in sight. With one hand they could literally each reach out and touch the vertical slopes of the Balangra La (Balangra pass), which was actual and real and devoid of subjective apprehensions. On the other hand was the psychic recognition of the featureless void beside them, along with an acute awareness that is often ejected into that uncreated expanse of space that lies beyond the distraction of dreams and memories, beyond the bend of bewildering mental afflictions, beyond the sway of yearning and temptation. It is a sudden acuity of awareness that calls the far-away mind to attention, compelling it to move beyond the pointless activities of life at a time when perseverance and purity of perception are imperative, a time when the enduring purpose of life should not be confused to the extent where one might be left empty-handed. Nevertheless, the gathering darkness eventually made it difficult for anyone to make out the contours of the natural surfaces with any kind of certainty, and so the men began to move more slowly, purposefully, with careful attention to each foot placement, and all three grouped up close behind Segunda, as the Gurkha appeared to be uniquely adept at finding his way forward along the narrow pass.

Finally, the trail widened as it circumscribed the shoulder of the mountain and descended to a lower altitude through an eerie forest of birch trees and conifers and oaks that were festooned with Spanish moss. The air was noticeably thicker and fragrant with the sweet honeysuckle and spicy nutmeg aromas of the late-blooming rhododendrons, mixed with fresh pine and juniper and the heady scent of wild roses. They made camp with a general feeling of security, knowing that no hostiles would be following behind them this particular evening, but there remained some serious apprehension as to what kinds of difficulties they were likely to encounter in the dangerous times to come.

Orion was glad that he had packed the camp stove and a goodly number of dehydrated meals, for they were soon feasting hungrily on beef teriyaki and chicken Polynesian as though it were the food of the gods, although each man seemed to exhibit his own personal preference regarding the structure and composition of a proper mountaineering spork. After the sumptuous rehydrated meal, Dahmer and LaFleche gathered around one particular pine tree and began to assemble a series of wires and a wire net at its base. Dahmer climbed up into the branches, carrying one of the wires about two-thirds of the way up to the top of the tree, and then he proceeded to hammer a nail into its trunk. LaFleche, with his squad radio, was soon in communication with HQ, which was able to patch him through to Captain Q. T. Umbrage, who briefed him on current operational strategies and intel and patched him through to Sergeant Bane. LaFleche provided Bane with some precise coordinates and promptly signed off to save batteries.

"That's a pretty neat trick," said Orion to LaFleche. "Does it work on any tree, or do you need a particular kind?"

"It's got to be a *live* tree," said LaFleche. "Dead trees don't work at all."

"You need to get the nail i.v. … into the sapwood," added Dahmer, and then he climbed into the tree again to retrieve both the wire and the nail.

As they were rolling their sleeping bags out onto the forest floor, Orion asked again about the tree antenna, "And where would someone learn a thing like that?"

"It's SOP, rookie … courtesy of the US Army Signal Corps Emergency Communications Manual."

The next morning, they started out early and continued west, moving out of the overgrown forests into a series of broad meadows and increasingly wide valleys. They avoided the caravans of nomads with their beastly overburdened yaks and slow-moving goats and sheep by trekking higher up the hillsides, passing quietly by the villages which appeared nearly uninhabited, guarded only by those spirit figures and the watchful Dok-pa (negativity averting) faces that peered at them from atop the houses, from among the heaps of freshly harvested grains and grasses that were stacked up high on the rooftops in anticipation of the coming snows that would soon close the mountain passes for the year, leaving these remote villages completely isolated from the outside world once again.

From a distance, it was difficult to discern which of the nomads and the few villagers they spotted might be practitioners of the Hindu,

Buddhist, or the shamanistic Bön religion. And given the interfusion of provincial archetypes and the broad profusion of headgear sported by the locals—ranging from colorful woolen scarves and balaclavas, to turbans of varying types, to Nehru hats and animal skins—such classical anthropological distinctions did little to narrow the field. However, the only headdress that mattered to this particular group of wilderness trekkers—the headdress that would assuredly supersede any and all forms of religiosity—was the distinctive Mao-style caps and headbands of the People's Army at large.

Moving down to the river through a grove of walnut trees, they came upon the ruins of a school compound and a schoolhouse with boarded-up windows and doors. Like all the other educational institutions that had been visited by the People's War, there were no children left to be seen or heard in this particular schoolyard.

"The pretty ones were either sold off to the traffickers for money or traded for military supplies," said LaFleche as he kicked in the doorway of the schoolhouse and peered inside at the empty classroom. Turning back to face Orion and the others, he began to pace the schoolyard in long, thoughtful strides. "Those would be the ones that the army stopped at the Indian border." He pivoted around and continued. "Most of the young men and boys will have been interned in indoctrination camps by now, being taught how to point and shoot, and the boys who are too small to shoot will be used as porters or message carriers, or worse, as human shields." LaFleche placed a wad of chewing tobacco into his mouth and adjusted its position with careful consideration, and then he continued pacing with long, muscular strides. "Those would be the ones that Bane and the Sherpa done gone and *relocated*."

The other men, who were resting comfortably with the weight of their packs removed, seemed content just to listen to the informative rant.

"And then there are the ones that are simply too beautiful or politically connected or ransom-worthy to be ignored—or all three, as in the case of Orion's beauty queen. In this rare and precious situation, we're dealing with both a *physical* and a *conceptual* mission which calls for a well-placed headshot," said LaFleche. "Don't you agree, Dahmer?"

"Couldn't agree more," said Dahmer, who after explicit prompting from Orion explained that a *conceptual mission* is a plan to take out the leaders or main power source that motivates something onward, and that a *headshot* is a single operation that renders the rest of an enemy's operation useless.

"Oh, it's a *conceptual mission* of headhunting and extrajudicial assassination," said Orion sarcastically. "And here I was thinking you guys were just bounty hunters."

Suddenly, the distinctive sound of a twin-engine Hip-H transport filled the valley as the profile of the giant helicopter appeared over the ridge top.

"Here comes Bane with our care package—right on time!" shouted LaFleche.

Sweeping across the valley without landing, the helicopter made its way slowly in the direction of their position while LaFleche, Dahmer, Segunda, and Orion frantically waved their arms and parkas in the air. The chopper appeared to be correcting its course for a low drop through an open door, when the sharp cracks of rifle shots rang out from the surrounding hillsides and the chopper veered up and away from their location. The shots continued with an increasing rate of fire, as the chopper continued to climb. A parachute appeared and floated downward in the prevailing wind—not toward the position of the deep reconnaissance patrol but away from their position, landing in a potato field a considerable distance away. The helicopter did not hang around to see where the shots were coming from, nor where the care package landed.

The men took cover behind a stone wall as the rifle shots were now being aimed in their direction, as evidenced by the small puffs of dust that were suddenly appearing in the schoolyard and by the sounds of bullets ricocheting off the stone wall. Dahmer and LaFleche had armed themselves with their fancy handguns, but they were rapidly being flanked from both sides; without cover fire, they were barely able to get off a single well-aimed shot. To the blind, every sound is sudden; to the terrified, everything happens way too fast. As Orion tried to press himself up closer against the stone wall, he heard the voice of Segunda speaking to him over the surrounding din.

"They are coming for you," he said in a calm, steady voice. "They are coming to take you to the firing squad, or perhaps it will be the gallows. Maybe they will break your bones and skin you alive out of spite. Or maybe they will simply burn you at the stake. You feel like you want to stand up and fight, but somehow you can't. Your mind is frozen with fear, and your body has entered a corpselike state; you are terrified of this awareness and your immediate separation from this cumbersome body of flesh and blood that has become too heavy to move. You would like to be able to rise up and confront your fears with a semblance of dignity, but you can't. So they will have to come and drag you away, after all."

The shooters were coming out from the woods now, moving *en masse* down the grassy slopes. Others appeared to be crossing the fields in the direction of the unintended drop zone. "If those bastards get to that chute before we do, we're gonna be in for a long damn day!" shouted LaFleche with an urgency that renounced all confusion.

Orion naturally found himself responding to the predicament without further thinking. In a panic, he began to unlace his hiking boots in a most curious form of ritualistic divestment. He tore into his expedition pack for his lightweight trail-runners, frantically pulling out nearly all of the things he previously carried, when a bullet slammed into the wall right beside him, and he covered his face with his hands.

All the while, Segunda was speaking to him in his uncanny manner, in a remarkably calm, steady voice: "Or is *it* coming to take you to your doom? And what about the others? Can you strive to take shelter in this cell-like space, out of harm's way, leaving it to others to fend off the chaos and the terror that surrounds you now, leaving it to others who are better trained to cope with the present state of emergency? Do you truly feel safe, Orion, or do you somehow feel trapped?"

Orion was shaking terribly now as he quickly donned and tied his running shoes tight with practiced precision. He frantically surveyed the scene as though everything was moving in slow motion. Dahmer and LaFleche were shooting and moving ever so slowly along the wall. The shooters were moving ever so slowly toward their position, and the sublime radiance of the sun was moving ever so slowly across the cloudless sky.

"You want to run, but your limbs are heavy; you want to break free, but you remain frozen in the languish of time, pretending that this is what you have decided to do."

But Orion told himself that this was not what he had decided; then he asked aloud a deeply personal question: *"What then must I do?"*

"You must face the true nature of appearances and illusion ... all the dissonant mental states that afflict you, all the self-originating thoughts that are conducive to the attainment of liberation, all the obstacles of malevolent forces and spirits that block your way—they too are not but the shadowy appearances of mind—"

And then Orion was up and running across the emptiness of the schoolyard, over the far wall, and out over the fields in a blaze of dramatic action. He was running like a man who was born to run like the wind and to travel at breakneck speed. All the years of training and conditioning and ski racing had come to his reserve. Tempered by the previous altitudes, hardened in his heartfelt resolve, and spurred to a fury by the unmitigated chemistry of fear itself, Orion sprinted out across the terraced fields in a hail of bullets and their reflected smithereens. He grabbed the parachute without so much as stopping and, in a shockingly original and impressively athletic maneuver, he hoisted the heavy carton up to his hip as he rolled into a sheltered ravine.

With his chest heaving for oxygen and his heart pounding hard in his chest, Orion ripped open the crate, pulled one of the tricked-out M4A1 carbines from its padding, and studied the array of contraptions—optical scope, light, laser pointer, etc. Apparently finding what he was looking for, Orion flipped the lever from SAFE to AUTO, slapped the curved magazine into place, racked and released the charging handle, and tapped the forward assist for good measure. He filled his pockets with extra magazines and emerged from the protection of the ravine with the assault rifle spouting lead as if there would be no tomorrow.

He sprayed the grassy slopes with an abandon known only to the truly terrified; only this time, everything was happening more slowly. He recalled, it seemed, the general locations of most of the shooters who were previously threatening them, instinctually recalling the direction of fire coming from the faceless menace—and he filled these spaces with lead. He reloaded intuitively, ergonomically, and he emptied magazine after magazine in the general direction of the hostiles, who were now running for their lives into the trees, and he continued to fire into the forests until Dahmer and LaFleche finally reached his position and LaFleche abruptly grabbed the weapon from his hands.

"What the hell are you doing, Orion! D'you think there's some kind of general store around here for us to buy more ammunition?"

Orion simply looked at Dahmer and LaFleche with wide-eyed amazement at his own autonomous actions. He stood hunched and panting with his hands by his sides, appearing clearly more ape than essence. He wasn't listening to the constructive criticism being actively voiced by LaFleche; rather, he was looking for Segunda, who was approaching the scene with the wry smile of a faithful guide, one who would not simply tell you what you wanted to hear, but what you actually needed to know.

"Damnedest thing I ever saw," complained LaFleche. "You're supposed to take aim once in a while before you empty the gun … what do you think about it, Dahmer?"

Dahmer was gazing up at the vultures who were already circling overhead, listening to the peaceful sounds of the river flowing and the wind as it swept through the pines. He walked up to the so-called rookie and gave him a friendly knuckle bump. "What do I think about it, you ask? I think that Orion has potential."

7.   The Third Bardo: Lord of Death

The men of the long range reconnaissance patrol packed up the new munitions and supplies in a hurry and moved out along the shallows of the river to a point where they plunged up to their waists into the icy water. They waded across some rapids among a causeway of partially submerged boulders, and then they headed up the mountainside to avoid what appeared to be an ominously deserted village beside the river. They climbed steadily for hours without stopping or speaking. They found a narrow foot trail and followed it up through a diminishing forest of pines and oaks and birch trees that were busy being strangled with Spanish moss, a scene of impending doom that was broken at times by patches of spent rhododendron flowers and the wilted stalks of wild lilies that had previously flowered and were now busy dying. The forlorn forest gave way to a series of low azalea bushes that were well past their summer blooms, and then these bushes gave way to windswept barrens as the men moved out across the exposed mound of a desolate mountain pass.

In the distance, the snow-covered summits of the Himalayas spread out in a magnificent panorama of physical form and function: *form* being that adamantine apex of solid determination which stands up against the relentless ravages of aging time, and *function* being that efficacy of indefatigable aspiration which emerges in and of itself.

They descended into the Tila Khola river valley through an

alternating series of patchy forests and grassy meadows while the daylight began to fade and deepening shadows crept across the landscape. As evening approached, they grouped up close and passed watchfully through a rustic hillside settlement that looked distinctively Tibetan in character. The thick, flat roofs of the primitive masonry houses were supported by a series of exposed beams that were crudely hewn and gray with age. Leaning up against the houses were squared-off logs into which steps were carved, providing access to the porches and the storehouse roofs. Some of the stone houses had been covered with white or brown stucco at some point in time, and the windows and doors showed faint remnants of what was once red and green paint; but the coverings were now severely weathered with the harshness of the seasons, and the inhabitants of these primitive abodes did not appear to be the least bit concerned about such a thing as curb appeal. There was a maze of stone walls which provided protected alcoves for barnyard animals and the storage of firewood and building lumber. Behind a stone wall and through an open doorway, the few existent villagers stared blankly, silently at this strange group of wilderness trekkers who, like civilization itself, was deliberately passing them by.

That night, they camped close to a stream at a place where the river valley widened into a magnificent amphitheater of alpine meadows. They dined hungrily on military MREs (Meals Ready-to-Eat) kindly provided by Sergeant Bane, et al., which included assorted main-course entrées, crackers or bread, commercial candy or fortified dessert, spreads of cheese, peanut butter or jelly, powdered beverage mixes of fruit-flavored drink, cocoa, coffee, tea, or dairy shake, and accessory packs of various seasonings, water-resistant matches, napkins, TP, and chewing gum—each unit also included a flameless ration heater to warm the main meal. While there was considerable bartering and haggling over the random assortment of auxiliary items allocated in the various MREs, there was a general uniformity of opinion concerning the cheap plastic spoon that was included with each individual meal *vis-à-vis* the aforementioned collection of personalized sporks.

Orion savored his chicken pasta Parmesan with crackers and fruit punch and then set out to filter more drinking water from the stream while Dahmer and LaFleche set up the radio antenna in a nearby pine tree to touch base with Bane and/or HQ, and Segunda left on his own to reconnoiter the enemy's proximity to their position. With clean water and provisions secured, it was determined that they were ready to move out fast if need be.

LaFleche poured some of the bottled water onto his shaved head and neck, and he explained to Orion that it was clear that they were on the right track, given certain information that was, shall we say, *extracted* from the human traffickers captured at the Indian border, and this *intel* was corroborated by the inspection of an abandoned bus that had been driven to the road's end near Sanfebagar in the Achham District. Apparently, Sergeant Bane and the Sherpa Outré had successfully deployed with the Royal Nepalese Army up at Simikot, thereby blocking any escape into Tibet to the north.

"In effect, what we've got is a funnel made of the Byasrikh and Changla Himal," LaFleche continued, referring to the two giant mountains through which their quarry must travel. He explained that the mountains would serve as the flanks of a strategic pincer maneuver that would funnel the high-value Maoist targets, the remaining kidnapped schoolgirls, and the American beauty queen right into the Royal Nepali Army and the secretive security force that was stationed at the northwest corner of Nepal, and which was now guarding the border and any escape into Tibet.

"You with me?" LaFleche's steely gaze met Orion's.

When Orion nodded, LaFleche went on. The only problem with the plan was that the evolving People's War was gradually progressing into new areas of high altitude and intrigue, which were totally devoid of any stabilizing influences of civilization. While the vast wilderness of Dolpo was generally considered to be the *wild west* of Nepal where the Maoists first created a stronghold, the high deserts of Humla in the far western region had more recently become a focus of the insurgency. With the exception of the police post and army barracks at Simikot, the entire district of Humla was rapidly falling into the hands of the Maoists. Isolated and remote, neglected by the government and nearly all development authorities, and bereft of any form of modern infrastructure, the impoverished Humla region in the far northwest corner of the besieged country was fast becoming a battlefield of the nation's civil war—and they were heading into its epicenter.

Segunda returned to the camp and informed the group—in his characteristic manner—that the men of the deep reconnaissance patrol wouldn't have to worry, at least for a while. They gathered some wood and built a small fire as the darkness closed in around them. Orion handed Segunda a titanium mug full of piping hot tea, and then Segunda moved off into the shadows to keep watch over the trail.

"That Gurkha sure has an unusual way of communicatin' his point of view," said LaFleche as he fastidiously melted the bowl of a plastic spoon over the coals of the fire.

"It takes some getting used to," acknowledged Orion. "But I must say, he sure has his moments … and I'm beginning to develop a kind of fondness for his guidance."

"You mean his guidance on the sheer cliffs at night or his guidance in your ear?"

"Both, I guess," said Orion, nodding thoughtfully as he answered. "No, definitely … it would *have* to be *both*."

"Yo, Orion," said Dahmer. "What was he saying to you right before you went ballistic back there at the drop zone?"

"It's kind of hard to describe to another person. I mean, it wasn't really personal, as I recall—it was more like he was informing me of the true reality of the situation and prompting me to make some kind of decision.…"

"Whatever it was he was saying to you must have been pretty exciting," said LaFleche. "Damnedest, most *unhealthy* thing I ever saw." LaFleche looked like he was about to spit on the ground to emphasize his point, but he had run out of chewing tobacco, and so he just shook his head.

Orion pulled out the crinkled photograph of Joycelyn and the children, which he had recovered from the schoolhouse at the Khumjung Sherpa village, and he passed it over to LaFleche, who studied it in the glow of the firelight and passed it over to Dahmer.

"I can see why you might want to get her back, that's for sure," said LaFleche, "but she looks too squeaky clean for me."

"Not likely to be doing much pole dancing," added Dahmer as he handed the photo back to Orion. "I, myself, like 'em good and nasty."

"And what about you, LaFleche?" asked Orion. "What is it that you look for in a woman?"

"Me, I look for *fear*," was his unabashed answer, and he said it with a flattened affect that suggested it might actually be true.

The men sat together in silence, watching the hypnotic flames of the campfire as they fluctuated entrancingly in the gusts of the cool evening breezes. They were all physically tired enough to sleep standing up, but their minds were still reeling from the drama of their narrow escape, and they were not yet ready for slumber.

"Tell me, Deadly Do-Right," said LaFleche abruptly, "now that you have been formally initiated into our little band of brothers, tell us what life is like in your neck of the woods. Tell us what it's like to be a national ski patroller out on a civilian search-and-rescue mission."

"Do you really want to know, or are you just being sarcastic?"

"I mean it, man. Tell us your favorite story about a ski rescue mission that went bad or something—something badass that we might be able to relate to."

"Yeah, tell us something really dark and scary that we can relate to."

"I don't think you guys are serious enough for me to even bother, and it's too bad."

"No, really, dude, I promise you that we will be all ears. Come on, man, you've got a captive audience."

Orion thought about it for a while. And then he rose to his feet, placed several large sticks onto the wuthering campfire, and began to tell his story.

"When I was a younger man, just out of college, I joined the National Ski Patrol, mostly so that I could keep on skiing every day—that, and the fact that I could never see myself as a coach or ski instructor. Well, we were traveled around quite a bit in the Outdoor Emergency Care program, learning about mountaineering practices, avalanche rescue, and toboggan handling, in addition to emergency medical procedures and the safe handling and delivery of trauma victims. As I recall, it was around Christmastime, and I found myself stationed up at Heavenly Valley in California. The weather conditions there were generally mild, and there was a moderate amount of very decent snow.

"Now, most of the time, it was just the usual thing: minor sprains and bruises on the 'bunny slopes' and gentle 'blue groomers' of this well-manicured Lake Tahoe ski resort. However, there is one part of the mountain that is not so 'cute' and 'cuddly,' in the terms of your paramilitary parlance. I am referring to the infamous 'steeps' on the far side, the Nevada side of the mountain, where every run is a double black diamond and 'EXTRA CAUTION' is advised in big red letters on the trail maps. To get to the far side, you first have to enter the windswept expanse of the Milky Way Bowl, where you immediately begin to realize that you have forsaken the familiar terrain of Heavenly Valley, with its graceful and majestic Jeffrey pines, for a foreboding landscape at the edge of the Nevada territory, a place where the mountain hollows out severely, where the icy slopes funnel and fall away in sheer walls and a sad, misshapen breed of pine trees struggles to hold on against the relentless forces of gravity and serious erosion.

"At the end of the day, it is important to patrol these areas before sundown, because no matter how difficult the visibility becomes at dusk, no matter how treacherous the skiing becomes when the sunlit snow turns back to ice, there is always some hotdog who is trying to squeeze just one more pristine run out of his lift ticket; and more often than not, such industrious souls tend to venture out alone."

Orion paused for a moment to tend the fire and to make sure his captive audience was still with him.

"Well, we traversed the expanse of the Milky Way Bowl all right—which takes some doing with the cumbersome weight of the toboggans—and we descended down through the funnel of the bowl to the control gate at the entrance of the Mott Canyon Cliffs as the sun was setting low behind us, casting long, gray shadows across the slopes from the hulks of the twisted trees. In a place like this, you'd think that a warning sign might mean something. The gate is marked with a great big sign displaying two black diamonds and the designation 'SUPER EXPERTS ONLY,' along with the warning: 'THIS AREA CONTAINS STEEP CHUTES, CLIFFS AND UNMARKED OBSTACLES.' Even the names of the ski runs should be enough to give pause to the foolish and the faint of heart—names like 'Pipeline!' 'Hemlock!' 'Widowmaker!' 'Snakepit!' 'Rocky Point!'—names like that are always fairly descriptive of the ski runs, suggesting that you might not want to trifle with them when the going gets dark.

"We swept past the most hazardous areas on a trail around Rocky Point and on into Promised Land, and we were about to board the chairlift out of the canyon when I noticed what looked like a body lying in a coffin right there on the upper slope to my left. I mean it! There was this young boy just lying there in a hollow depression in the snow, and in the gathering gloom, it looked like he was lying in some kind of stone-cold sarcophagus.

"The boy was barely conscious and obviously in deep shock, and you could tell by the long, smearing trail of blood on the slope that he had somehow managed to drag himself down through the reaches of Snakepit to get to the point where someone like me might see him. Gazing up at the cliff he had just come down, it looked to me more like a frozen waterfall than a skiable run—and I'm telling you this from my point of view as an experienced downhill ski racer. Looking down at the unnatural angle of his right leg, I could tell right away that it was broken badly above the knee at the level of the thigh."

On his feet still, Orion bit his lower lip softly and crouched low on his haunches. "I'm telling you all this," he said softly but fiercely, "because it is important for you to know that this was one brave and determined kid. Not only was he naturally adventurous and relatively fearless in his death-defying pursuit of such youthful endeavors, he had to have a considerable amount of skill to even get himself into this situation, let alone get himself down the icy cliffs of Snakepit with a badly broken leg. After we radioed for emergency services, we splinted his leg and bundled him into the toboggan. The thing I remember most about that particular dim and darkening day was the way he grabbed hold of my arm. The boy was deep in shock and barely conscious, as far as I could tell, but he raised his head and he clutched my forearm with a trembling, almost palsied desperation. He reached out, trembling with the courage of hope and expectation—though I could tell he was struggling and shivering with some unmistakable awareness: that for *him*, the worst was yet to come. To this day, I can still recall that shivering grip upon my arm."

Orion paused and shuddered with the recollection, and then he continued.

"Now, what's so bad about a broken leg, you ask, it happens all the time. We've all seen far worse things in our lives, in car accidents and earthquakes and plane crashes; and for you operators, it would be in any given war. And I'll leave those kinds of stories for guys like you to tell. But this would turn out to be an entirely different kind of natural disaster, a different kind of horror, a different kind of battle in a different kind of war.

"Yes, indeed, he broke his leg. It's true to a certain extent. But behind this simple truth is a deeper, darker aspect of reality, a truth of the most outrageous and destructive sort, a truth that assails the fortified pillars of our consciousness as it wreaks havoc on our dreams and pierces the very fabric of our being. It is a truth that is among the most difficult to accept, and yet it is also among the most perilous to deny …. This truth is that our flesh and bones are prone to grievous errors on the inside, and if this sad truth be told, there is no honest ounce of prevention, and few, if any, cures.

"It turned out that the strain of the steeps and the giant bumps of Snakepit only served to uncover a far more insidious problem with the boy's leg. Apparently, that adolescent growth plate, that very mass of cellular anlagen that causes young men and women to grow straight and tall and strong of limb in the years to come, and which heals their accidental breaks and wounds time and time again, had just perchance—through an iota of grievous error—given rise to a form of cancer that had weakened his thigh bone and would ultimately threaten his life.

"It started out as a simple error, a brief miscue of genetic code—nothing anyone would notice. A simple error, and then another—nothing much to worry about, nothing to lose any sleep over. It could happen to anyone, really, at any time at all, on any day in any place, in any of the living tissues within our bodies, be it blood or bones or glands or bowels. Yet as we live and breathe and strive, unaware of the growing darkness within us, the grievous error begins to multiply in increasing numbers as it mounts an insidious assault upon the tranquil landscapes of our physical being.

"It turned out he was a pretty cool kid, and I kept in touch with his progress, from emergency services and intensive care through limb salvage surgery, ionizing radiation, and standard chemotherapy and all the marvels of modern medicine. They gave him a titanium rod in place of his diseased femur, and he was doing pretty well with the physical therapy. We were all thinking that he would be off to the races and back to school in no time at all.

"But no. That would not be a story worth telling at such a time and place as this. You wanted to know why I do what I do, why I hunt with the intention of rescue. You wanted to hear about patrols gone bad, when things get dark and scary. Well, this is my story, for better or worse. And it means a lot to me. But I can stop right here if you're tired of listening ..."

"Hell no," said LaFleche. "You've gone to a lot of trouble to make us care about this tragic kid. The least you could do is to tell us why we should!"

"Uhh yeah, dude," agreed Dahmer, "you gotta finish the story *properly.*"

"Okay, you convinced me. But as you might have guessed, the worst was yet to come. Of course, the cancer returned with a vengeance, as cancers are prone to persist; and try as they might … try as they could … try as they were taught, there was nothing the doctors could do. There was nothing in the clinical oncologists' medicine cabinet that could stand up to the relentless onslaught of the metastatic spread, once the first blush of efficacy had come and gone and the cancer had become chemotherapy-resistant. It would start out as a simple numbness or a lump here or there, a swollen gland or two; it was by a twitch or a wince or an alarming pain that it made its presence known.

"Certainly, there were treatments: more surgery and ionizing radiation and tinctures of poisons, defoliants, nerve gas, heavy metals, and radiation—you know, all the readily available implements of modern warfare—but nothing did one bit of evidence-based good. Nothing invented in the past hundred years could even halt the progression. I visited him several times in the hospital, and each time was worse than the last. I actually had to steel myself to face the horror of the vision of decrepitude that would rise up and confront me physically—the vision of a helpless human being still trying to be cheerful in the process of being eaten alive.

"The side effects of these noxious yet ineffectual treatments were horrific, causing severe damage to the boy's marrow, and nerves, and liver, and even his sinking heart. He was poisoned and burned and nearly cut to pieces; his chest was opened on several occasions to remove bloody masses of errant tissue. But there was nothing that could truly be done; there was no cure, and somehow, he knew that from the very beginning—I'm almost sure of it now. It was that very same boy who once grabbed a quivering hold of my arm up at Heavenly Valley, but he was no longer of this world. A slow death with ice-cold hands had laid his weary bones in a living tomb—you gotta pity the devastations that this gnawing death hath made as you survey the millions by its arms confined. I know *now* what he was trying to tell me then—that though he, himself, was surely doomed, he wanted his struggle to matter."

Orion gazed across the firelight into the shining faces of Dahmer and LaFleche.

"It may not mean a lot to you guys, but this boy fought like a soldier. He hung on through all the standard treatments, hung on as the cancer spread to his spleen and his lungs and his liver and his brain. He said he wanted to play some part in the development of a cure, not only for himself, but for others like him. He offered to take part in an experimental treatment that used a monoclonal antibody that might or might not fight the tumor, but what it did for certain, at the doses required, was to saturate every possible nerve fiber and leave him in screaming pain. Eventually, encroaching masses in his neck began to press upon his spinal nerves as the progress of the cancer slowly paralyzed each of his limbs.

"Still, he was holding on with the hope there would be a better medicine that could fight *for* him—not against him—on the inside, where it counts. He told me that he was waiting for some kind of gene-based treatment that would be more selective for the disease itself, without so much collateral damage. He told me that modern science had the knowledge of genetics and the know-how to design the right kind of therapeutic payload to selectively destroy the cancer cells—I'm telling you, he was a pretty bright kid. But he said that they hadn't yet perfected the art of targeted gene delivery, and he was holding on for that.

"He knew that he would never ski again, or even run or walk. He would never know a single day of freedom from the dreadful disease that continued to grow and multiply at his expense. Still he hung on with courage and conviction, encouraging others by his example, encouraging others to care enough to help deliver the goods. You know, I think in some strange and wondrous way, the boy actually did accomplish something special … something that continued on and on, long after he died. I know that his plight encouraged me to dedicate my time and efforts to help to rescue the lost and the injured. But, more than that, I think he encouraged others to recognize that his terrible situation was not just an isolated problem but an intolerable state of affairs that should be worthy of mankind's best, most heroic efforts.

"In the end, one of the tumors in the boy's lungs eroded a bronchial artery, and he drowned in his own blood. But you know, it was not long after that dark night when one of the medical groups that were treating the boy actually came up with a practical delivery system, and there are people still alive today as a result of it. And it's a good thing too, because the more I learned about metastatic cancer from this particular search-and-rescue mission, the more I realized that the same thing could happen to any one of us at any given moment on any given day or night."

Judging from the silence that followed, it appeared that the paramilitary men at the campfire were unusually thoughtful. These men, who were accustomed to facing life and death on their own terms, seemed to be genuinely unnerved by the contemplations; which was strange, considering that they did not appear to be the least bit affected when they were exchanging small-arms fire with a Maoist army brigade.

The unattended campfire had burned down to embers. In the silence of the evening, they could hear the resonant voice of Segunda, who was situated nearby in the darkness.

"Oh death, oh death, won't you pass me over for another year."

It sounded like something that was ancient and yet familiar, something between an Old English broadside ballad and an Appalachian dirge.

"Oh death, oh death, won't you pass me over for another year."

The daylight came on dreary through a heavy, overbearing mist that obscured everything in the far distance but the upper curve of the big, dull, reddish-orange ball that rose ever so slowly over the treetops. The men of the long range reconnaissance patrol moved out through the dripping alpine meadows on a trail to the northwest with the greatly diminished sun and the last dying breaths of the seasonal monsoon at their backs. The summer verdancy of the tree-lined pastures was muted now; the once-bright orchids, buttercups, wild geraniums, and cheerful forget-me-nots that spangled and adorned the grassy meadows earlier in the year appeared sallow and depressed, as if weakened by the loss of some invigorating spirit. The addition of atmospheric moisture to the rarefied air heightened the senses as it awakened the mind to the musky aromas of the surrounding fields and forests and the distinctive smells of a herd of rangy goats that scrubbed against their pants as they were mustered by with their jingling bells and their little saddlebags filled with freshly harvested grains. The deeply weathered faces of the goatherds and their jangling drove of beasts passed by the line striving men as in a dream that faded rapidly into the mist, and then the euphonious sounds of the tiny bells faded away as well, leaving only the jingle-jangle memories of the close encounter in the vaporous morning.

The crunching sounds of the men's own hurried footsteps were accompanied by the ceaseless murmur of water moving swiftly beside them, dashing over and around all obstacles in a tireless, relentless rush to reach some final destination. They headed down-valley and crossed the river single file on a quaking cantilever bridge that was held together tenuously by a series of large wooden pegs. Moving with urgency past the remote outcroppings of stone huts that defined one impossibly rustic village after another, the men of the deep reconnaissance patrol were met with the typical pastoral sounds of women at work in the agricultural extremities of western Nepal.

The rhythmic seasonal cycles of these rugged female inhabitants were punctuated by the repetitive percussions of their daily routines. In the foreground, groups of women were at work chopping firewood for the winter. On the flattened stage of a nearby rooftop, silhouetted by the uniform grayness of the sky, there were women at work thrashing grains; on another elevated stage, the women were busy with thick poles, pounding rice or barley into flours. Orion imagined Joycelyn Eberhard on yet another stage, one with the pounding of applause rising in increasing adoration.

Suddenly, as the men emerged from a narrow canyon and worked their way up into the expanse of another broad, unsettled valley, there emerged much coarser sounds and harsher percussions—startling, thumping sounds of an entirely different order. The thunderous percussions stopped the lead members of the reconnaissance patrol in their tracks, wresting Orion from his reverie and sending Segunda and LaFleche to the nearest rock outcroppings for cover. The men grouped up and squatted down without removing their packs.

"Sounds like socket bombs," said Dahmer to LaFleche, who nodded affirmatively.

"Sounds like lots of 'em, as far as I can tell. It sounds to me like Jumla itself might be under attack."

"What's a socket bomb?" asked Orion as he tensed from the echo of a particularly loud explosion.

"It's a crude, homemade explosive device made from water pipe fittings with threaded plugs screwed onto the ends," explained Dahmer. "It's easy enough for anyone to assemble—the only trouble being the fusing and/or tamping on the detonator cap without blowing one's own head off."

"Which many of the damn-fool Maoists simply fail to do," added LaFleche. "Still, I wouldn't want to be on either the heaving or the receiving end of those blasted kitchen grenades."

The distant percussions increased in frequency to such an extent that it sounded like the finale of a holiday fireworks display. Segunda promptly headed up the hillside in the general direction of the explosions. The others followed him up to a small pass and out across the exposed ridge of a mountainside that overlooked the rivers and the district headquarters of Jumla, with its charming rice terraces and water-powered mills. Situated in a fertile valley at the confluence of two meandering rivers, flanked by acres of grain fields and rice paddies, and embraced by the gentle folds of green coniferous mountains, the terraced farmlands of Jumla might be considered idyllic, were it not for the waves of furious insurgents presently assaulting the central village and the thunderous concussions of grenades and gunfire and the acrid plumes of thick black smoke that were emanating from the outlying houses and administrative buildings.

Orion crouched down with the others on the overlooking ridge and squinted hard into the distance. Out in front of the uniformed insurgents wearing mottled camouflage fatigues, he could make out a more diminutive human wave of attackers that was more variably attired in civilian clothing and appeared to be much, much younger in age. As he watched in horror and amazement, Orion could see that a great number of these little people were being cut down by gunfire coming from protected military positions as they attempted to run across the grain fields. Many of the young people appeared to be carrying the aforementioned socket bombs, while others appeared to be wielding only wooden spears and assorted farm implements. Those who managed to get close to the barricades were caught up in the barbed wire, others were cut down or blown up in the process, and few, if any, were able to get close enough to the main government buildings to do much damage. Watching the struggle of the young "military personnel" caught on the barbed wire, Orion could feel his own stomach turn. He had often heard the term *cannon fodder* used in polite conversation, but until today, he had never imagined that he would witness the horrifying phenomenon with his own eyes; nor had he imagined how deeply and thoroughly disturbing it would be.

"Those are just children being slaughtered out there!" shouted Orion. "Isn't there anything we can do to stop this?" he said as he suddenly stood up, slid off his expedition pack, and grabbed hold of LaFleche's sleeve.

LaFleche simply clasped Orion's thumb and skillfully twisted it in such a manner as to bring Orion expediently to his knees, and then he released it with a downward flourish of his palm that said, *Stifle it, and keep down with the rest of us to avoid detection.* Then LaFleche pointed two fingers to his own eyes and then to the battlefield as he spoke softly and frankly. "Watch and learn Orion," he said, "There are more of those children and their Maoist handlers down there than there are Royal Army bullets in that compound. And anyway, it's not our fight."

Orion nodded his head in reluctant acceptance, as he fully realized his inexperience in such matters, and then he looked over expectantly to Segunda, who had moved in close by his side.

"You always need to be mindful of your own personal mission. You need to be mindful that this is a war that will go on forever; this is a cycle of monstrous ambition drenched in bloody hatred; this is a war that no one will ever win."

Orion reeled with the dreadful excitation, the great uncertainty of his position, the ongoing tragedy playing out before him, the frustration of stifling his natural emotions, and the wisdom of these prescient revelations, and he watched in awe and wonder as he struggled to attain a calmer, more abiding state of mind.

The drama of the battle intensified as wave after wave of child soldiers advanced upon the compound, forcing the Royal Nepalese Army to abandon its positions and fall back to some makeshift fortifications located near a small airstrip. The child soldiers, with their primitive weapons and their sacks of socket bombs, formed a human shield of exaggerated dimensions and unnatural appearances and moved at great expense and loss of life into the administrative center of the village, where streams of black smoke began to rise from building after building. Soon, the older uniformed Maoists advanced behind this human shield and disappeared into the larger buildings while the child soldiers were reinforced by hundreds of others who were now crossing the rivers, moving through the grain fields, and converging upon the scene.

Eventually, the wave of youthful insurgents reached the airstrip, setting fire to the single-story control tower building and assaulting the last remnants of resistance as the automatic weapon fire diminished. One could only imagine what happened to the last Nepali soldiers who attempted to surrender, for there was no quarter to be found on this disconsolate day.

All this time, Dahmer was constantly scanning the chaotic military operation through the lens of his tricked-out M4A1 carbine. He appeared to be following the movements of one particular group of Maoists who had not taken part in the assault on Jumla and yet were now streaming, with a good number of porters carrying baskets like a line of industrious ants, beyond the district headquarters to the north.

"I think I found our bad guys, dudes. Those baskets are definitely not filled with red rice or barley."

"Do you see any major operators coming up from the southeast?" asked LaFleche. "I can't imagine that our schoolgirls walked all the way from those abandoned buses in the Achham district and got here before we did."

"There are some beat-up jeeps down there with the well-dressed bad guys, which tells me something about that. So my best guess is that our high-value targets already moved past this point without getting their hands dirty and that these high-value looters will lead us right to them."

Orion strained to view the northern landscapes, looking for any sign of hostages.

"You *do* know that there are two different passages to the north that lead to Rara Lake?" said Segunda in a manner that was considerably more rhetorical than inquisitive.

"Right you are, Segunda Gurkha," said LaFleche. "And we can choose to take the proverbial road less traveled by."

Suddenly, the overcast sky grew darker. Like something from a nightmare, the clouds roiled and took macabre shapes that, when Orion focused, became helicopter gunships. Bright flashes erupted steadily from the crafts, and the pattering of spewing machine guns filled the air. Down below, the insurgents began to scatter and take cover as the machine guns opened up on every living thing in sight. Again and again, the gunships swept down upon the Maoist army with lethal repercussions. The insurgents were mowed down in the grain fields; they were butchered in the rice paddies. Even as they streamed in terror across the bridges and the shallows, they were targeted one by one and eliminated in a hail of machine-gun fire. Then, as quickly as the gunships had arrived, the retaliatory strike force was gone.

Orion rubbed his eyes, attempting at some subconscious level to erase the terrifying visions that lay before him in the cold, gray, hazy mist below. When he took his hands away, the visions remained. The land was littered with a gruesome autumn harvest—sheaves of human corpses. Motionless bodies floated in the slowly moving waters like newly fallen leaves.

As the men of the long range reconnaissance patrol moved out along the ridgeline to their intended destination in the north, Orion felt a profound sense of gloom descending upon his mind like ancient mists that gathered and clung to the low places, making his legs feel heavy as though he were moving in drying cement, clouding his thoughts with a vaporous miasma of reluctance, ambiguity, and dismay. He glanced back at the surreal scene, feeling as though he were leaving something important behind.

Dahmer must have sensed Orion's level of situational confusion, for he offered a note of sympathy when he passed by and nudged Orion's shoulder with his elbow. "Don't worry about it, Orion … it's just the fog of war."

8.   Mirror of Karma

The next two days, they traveled fast and well into the night, moving on their chosen path of hardship, sacrifice, difficulty, and danger, pressing further into the realms of ceaseless pain and hunger. They were driven by an ever-increasing sense of doom and propelled onward by an urgency that seeks to find a way through paths where Byron's wolves would fear to prey, stopping only for hydration, an occasional MRE, or to take care of pedal hot spots and blisters with Moleskin, new skin, second skin, and/or duct tape. They pushed on hard, ascending steadily through clusters of blue pine trees into wide alpine meadows rising up to the north. Breathing became noticeably harder and faster and deeper as the team worked their way up through rocky terrain to the windy summit of a high mountain pass, marked by tattered prayer flags and a crude stone chorten. Beyond the summit, the snow-white peaks of the Changla Himal surged up into a clear blue sky.

Following a narrow trail across the top of the ridge, the men worked their way down the mountainside through a patchy coniferous forest, which eventually gave way to grassy meadows and stands of magnificent birch trees that were presently divesting themselves of the season's quivering leaves; leaves that were shimmering brightly in their amber autumn colors only to waft away in great numbers upon the gusts of the crisp mountain breezes and then flutter and tumble down to the ground. The less-traveled foot path descended more steeply now as it led along rocky cliffs into the valley of the Sinja Khola, dropping through walnut forests and bamboo groves all the way down to the floor of the valley, where the men crossed over the surging river by means of an expansive cantilever bridge. At this point, LaFleche and Dahmer held a tactical meeting and decided that it would be a good idea to blow up the bridge.

"Roger that," said Dahmer, unshouldering his pack nonchalantly. He leaned out and surveyed the supporting structures of the wooden bridge. "Shouldn't be a problem making toothpicks out of these old timbers."

Orion, who had followed Segunda farther up the trail, doubled back to the river bank, where he pumped some filtered drinking water into his empty bottles and passed them around in exchange for more empties, which he filled in the same manner. All eyes now turned to Dahmer, who had placed a series of canvas-covered charges against the outstretched supports of the cantilever structure. He then linked the dual-primed charges with detonation cord and nonelectric firing assemblies.

"Yo, D-man," shouted LaFleche from the edge of the bridge.

"Right here, bro," responded Dahmer without looking up.

"What is your time delay?"

"One minute, give or take …"

"You may proceed when ready," said LaFleche with a great big smile as he backed away from the bridge.

"Burning!" shouted Dahmer, grabbing his pack and scrambling off the rickety wooden bridge in a hurry. The pace at which Dahmer exited the scene encouraged the others to follow suit.

They were all still running—and, if truth be told, they were laughing—when the detonation caps and explosive charges went off with a deafening staccato blast that thundered through the river valley, while the outbound remains of the old wooden bridge showered the entire area with a cloud of splinters and smithereens. Looking back at the ruined bridge, Orion gradually realized that, in addition to thwarting any enemies that might have lurked behind them, he had just passed a critical and dramatic point of no return. Judging from the animated expressions of his paramilitary colleagues, it appeared that the other men of the deep reconnaissance patrol had just realized this too.

The trail followed along the riverbed, and they hiked for more than an hour before rising up at the approach to what appeared to be an abandoned village of stone houses, and then they continued single file along the side of the mountain about two hundred meters above the river. They passed another village which also appeared to be deserted, but which left each member of the reconnaissance patrol with the uncanny feeling that they were being watched. They moved with the contours of the river valley in an increasingly westward direction, fording several small streams that entered the main river from the north, skirting yet another mysteriously vacant outcropping of crude houses, and heading up, down, and up again along the narrow footpaths cut into the steep rock walls.

From time to time, Dahmer and LaFleche would briefly pause to check their position on a topographical map by locating recognizable landmarks or by recording a directional azimuth attained by sighting through a lensatic compass and noting the bearings. More often than not, the men followed closely behind Segunda, who managed to navigate day or night with a keen sense of direction and terrain, all without the aid of applied trigonometry and the added precision of military mil-radian bearings.

The deep reconnaissance patrol moved evermore downrange, drawing closer to the anticipated position of the enemy insurgents by traversing west with the river valley, heading downstream now in the general direction of the archeological digs of Sinja, where they had plotted a strategic location for an ambush. Here, in the disenfranchised land of the ancient Malla Kingdom of the Karnali River basin, there once existed a "royal highway," as it were, in the twelfth to fourteenth centuries, and was historically a popular trade route stretching north from the Inner Terai Valleys through Jumla, past Rara Lake, and all the way up into Tibet. It was along this tortuous walking route that the high-value Maoist targets would undoubtedly be traveling with their ill-gotten booty, and it was here in this area of operation that the elite paramilitary members of the long-range reconnaissance patrol were planning to take direct action.

They moved through the long, hard days and nights, feeling increasingly remote and disconnected from the world around them. The hillside villages they passed by were either empty of any inhabitants or were completely wary of any intrusion, be it Maoist, Royalist, or even Protagonist disguised as a pedestrian backpacker. The alienation of the scraggly men in khaki pants and field jackets from their immediate surroundings was as palpable as it was complete. Unshaven and sunburned, Orion and his cadre no longer looked like a group of casual wilderness trekkers being led by a kindly Nepali guide; Orion was one among a resolute troupe of four hard guys with a uniform appearance of grave determination. Days and degrees of separation from anything and everything familiar had hardened his body and his mind. Together, they appeared more like ghosts on the trail than armed men moving upon the terra firma at a desperately urgent pace—four full-metal-jacketed bullets passing straight through the picture postcards of these vast and extraordinary landscapes.

When it grew too dark to move safely along the footpaths, they ate the remaining MREs, and LaFleche successfully made radio contact with Sergeant Bane, who was hunkered down comfortably with the Sherpa Outré and the Royal Nepalese Police Force in Simikot. Orion could hear LaFleche's side of the conversation while he was sorting out his sleeping gear. Although there was only minimal Maoist activity reported in the surrounding district, LaFleche assured Bane, and Captain Umbrage by proxy, that the bad guys would surely be heading that way.

When the night air grew colder, they bedded down in tents to avoid the gathering frost, keeping guard duty in two-man pairs. Each man was armed with a flashlight and an H&K Mark-23 handgun with its sound suppressor, laser aiming module, and chambered round ready to go. Bivouacking deep in no-man's land on operational deployment, and progressing downrange in a prospective combat zone, they were prepared to move out, to fight, or to fend off an attack at all times, in accordance with paramilitary SOP.

They broke camp in the vague twilight of daybreak and were on the trail toward Sinja village before sunrise. They moved silently now, and more cautiously, awakening with a prickly awareness of the prevalence of real danger and a sharp sense of catastrophe which eludes more privileged populations and nations. They maneuvered into a strategic position of protected high ground just north of the village of Botan at the confluence of two rivers, a position overlooking a steep, sinuous trail that led north from Sinja to Rara Lake along the crumbling and fragmented ridgeline of a precipitous mountain. LaFleche brought the patrol to a stop with an upward movement of his hand, drawing attention to the distant trail across the way by drawing a horizontal line in the air. Extending out and across the face of the mountain, the impossibly exposed route led up along the sheer cliffs of a spectacular gorge, making their selected location directly across the gorge appear like an ideal spot for an ambush. Looking across the gorge, Orion thought to himself that the mere sight of the precipitous drops off those sheer cliffs would be enough to frighten the average traveler to distraction.

LaFleche explained to Orion that the basic skill set required for a successful raid or an ambush was nearly the same, the main difference being the intents and purposes of the reconnaissance required. "In an ambush, where the target is moving, the recon is aimed at finding a suitable site from which to attack the moving target. A good ambush site—like the one we have here—is one in which the patrol can establish proper security for the strike team while providing a good field of fire to engage the enemy."

Orion surveyed the surrounding area and nodded with approval. "I, for one, can appreciate the advantages of high ground," he said.

"In a raid, where the target is stationary," continued LaFleche, "the quality of the reconnaissance is everything. In this case, you need to observe the target—his routine activities, numbers, weaponry, and physical defenses—well in advance of the raid in order to plan your method of attack."

Dahmer chimed in with his own pearls of wisdom: "In each case, we are looking for tactical surprise and violence of action," he said with an impish note of satisfaction.

Segunda appeared to be transfixed, staring off in the distance at what looked like the ruins of an ancient Hindu temple that was poised like a beacon, peaked and white, as though it were floating upon the top of a nearby precipice. Judging from the intensity of his facial expression and the yogic immobility of his posture, this particular temple must have held some deep and powerful spiritual meaning for the enigmatic Gurkha.

As the big orange ball crested the mountains in the east, a south-bound caravan of twenty-some yaks adorned with bells and bright red tassels and a half dozen yak-herders dressed in earth-tone garb entered the exposed theater of operations. Laden with large sacks of Tibetan rock salt, dried sheep meat, wool, carpets, and colorful blankets, the caravan of sure-footed yaks worked their way slowly down the narrow trail and across the exposed cliffs directly in view and in range of the ensconced ambush team. In the weeks to come, the same caravan might be carrying rice, tea, sugar, woven cloth, or kerosene on the return trip. There were no signs yet of the Maoists or their chain of porters moving in the opposite direction, and the deep reconnaissance patrol relaxed in anticipation of a potentially lengthy term of surveillance.

If only to pass the time in style, LaFleche, in a rare moment of camaraderie, encouraged Segunda to share his impressions of the faraway hilltop temple with the group: "What could possibly be so interesting about a bunch of tumbledown temple stones?"

"You would be pleased to know those tumbledown stones were once fierce lions that guarded the inner sanctum of Bhagwati Than," said Segunda calmly.

"Bag of what?" queried LaFleche.

Segunda did not respond; he just stared off in the distance at the temple knoll.

"Really, Segunda," encouraged Orion. "Tell us something about the narrative."

Segunda simply smiled and said, "If you truly think about it, you can remember a time when the gods and the legends were much closer to the world than they are today. You think about how you loved those exalted stories of drama and adventure as a kid. You can nearly sense the presence of those legendary heroes and heroines for a moment or two before they vanish into ancient memory." Then he closed his eyes and smiled that same smile. And then, without opening his eyes, Segunda began to speak in a manner that was even more inscrutable than usual: "Oh, what a singular moment is this, the first one, when you have hardly begun to recollect yourself … a drama revealed and remembered."

The others moved in closer to hear what he was saying whilst Segunda sat nearly motionless, smiling calmly with his eyes closed for several minutes. The men looked at each other with alternating expressions of curiosity, concern, and bewilderment. No one said a word.

Then, with everyone pressing near, Segunda's eyes suddenly snapped open, and his calm smile brightened at the sight of the men's blank faces. "By unclosing your eyes so suddenly, you can surprise the personages of your dream in full convocation—perchance to catch one broad glance at them before they flit into obscurity."

The men pulled back from the speaker in unison, each one shaking his head with an equal mixture of chagrin and relief.

"Funny guy," said Dahmer.

"Thought we lost you for a moment," said Orion.

"Must be some kind of Gurkha humor," said LaFleche, who was not entirely satisfied with the explanation of the temple mythos. "So, what's so secret about this tumbledown temple, other than the fact that it looks downright *inaccessible* to me?"

"You mean inaccessible, as in *invincible*, don't you?" responded Segunda.

"Well, yes. I'm a military man, after all," said LaFleche.

"It appears you know more about Durga, Avatar of Devi, than you realize."

"Can you explain it to me in English, for pity sake ... none of us mortals speak Sanskrit."

Segunda stared intently and unblinking into the distance, his eyes fixed on the sunlit glint of the temple ruins. "When you enter the gateway of the temple, you leave your ordinary thoughts behind. You become aware of the extraordinary mental and physical planes of a more exalted existence that is expressed architecturally in the massive and magnificent construction. Though it makes you feel so insignificant, you are drawn by the grand carvings and elaborate artistic decorations, and you proceed to move inward, removing your earthbound clodhoppers and directing your mind to seek that knowledge which your heart alone is capable of sensing."

The men gathered closer again to hear the exact words that Segunda was voicing to no one in particular.

"You enter into the darkness, forsaking the glaring light of day ... knowing that you've come a long way, and you've still got a long way to go ... knowing that you're bound to the hunt for something precious and rare which constantly eludes you in the daylight ... and so you enter into the darkness, forsaking the glaring light of day."

"The man's got a point," quipped LaFleche, "though I'll be damned if I can catch hold of it with all this daylight in the way."

"It sounds pretty circular to me," said Dahmer, who was busy adjusting the scope of his M4A1 assault rifle to the approximate distance of the cliff face. "Maybe you can catch the gold ring the next time around."

"Let the man speak," said Orion. "We're all busy hunting for something that we haven't even seen in quite a while. As far as I'm concerned, we can use all the celestial help we can get."

"As you enter further into the inner sanctum of the temple," continued Segunda, "the physical, mental, and spiritual worlds coalesce, and you can almost feel the presence of a great shining being—he who sparkles in her eyes, he who lights the heavens in the darkness, he who hides in the souls of all living creatures—and your awakened mind is focused on that divine presence like the dust of iron that gathers to a natural magnet. And it is here in the consummate darkness of the sanctum sanctorum, when a brave torch is lit and waved before the sacred deity, that you catch a glimpse of the image of Durga Bhagwati, Goddess of Victory and Vengeance, mounted atop a powerful tiger, armed with many arms and an abundance of weapons, ready, willing, and able to protect mankind once again from a reign of terror and the pain and suffering caused by evil forces."

"Hold on there, Segunda," interrupted LaFleche. "I might not be no *magna cum laude* when it comes to the philosophy of religions, but I do recall a thing or two from those Special Forces slide shows we had on Hindu cultural anthropology."

"Yeah, we learned, by sleeping, how to avoid *death by PowerPoint*," added Dahmer.

"Seriously, dudes," continued LaFleche. "It is my understanding that the Hindu religion is focused on three lords-a-leaping—that is, Brahma, Vishnu, and Shiva, and that the latter two are more than capable of protecting virtue and destroying evil in the world."

"Well, what about it, Segunda?" prompted Orion. "Is it those lordly guys or your Durga Goddess on a tiger that deserves top billing in the triumph of good over evil?"

Segunda continued to stare intently at the temple knoll, and though he appeared to be aware of the philosophical conversation going on around him, his mind had traveled far away from the scene of the ambush to another astral plane. The sun continued to rise in the sky. A small train of wooly sheep moving slowly along the cliffs across the gorge was narrowly passed by a group of three porters, each carrying a large woven basket on his back. Confident that the high-value targets were not yet in sight, Dahmer, LaFleche, and Orion turned their attention again to Segunda, who appeared to be deep in meditation.

"We don't mean to be rude, Segunda," offered Orion. "But we could sure use your help in preparing for the ambush. There are so few of us, and I'm afraid that we may be outmanned and outgunned if you aren't with us 100 percent. Is there anything that I can do to help you complete your meditations before the evildoers arrive?"

"When in the course of human events you encounter a terrible rise in demonic forces; when the suffering of the innocents, the mishandling of children, poverty, cruelty, injustice, and/or inequity increases to a point where it threatens the world; when evil forces arise as if to threaten the existence of the gods themselves, you must strive to contemplate an eternal truth: The sublime authority of the great gods alone is ineffectual apothecary for the chaotic situation at hand. The demons of uncontrolled strength and reckless pride remain both unvanquished and terrifying, with an army too many to count. Such demons cannot be uncreated, nor can they be defeated by the principal gods, who bear silent witness, and nor can such demons be defeated by appeals to their authorities."

"Sounds grim, Segunda," said LaFleche. "So what's your magic bullet?"

"In times like these, you need to remember the divine power of the supremely radiant Mother Goddess, or Durga. She is considered difficult to reach, or *inaccessible*, in her temple fortress, and yet she is empowered with the combined forces of all the primordial cosmic energies of the Divine Trimurti. She protects her beloved children with fierce compassion. In situations of utmost distress, she uses the many weapons at her command with fearlessness and patience, and she is virtually *invincible* in battles of epic proportions. It is Durga Bhagwati, the radiantly beautiful warrior goddess with her many arms and weapons, who slays the terrible buffalo demon and his army."

"You mean that the three lords-a-leaping are abstract to the point where they can't lift a finger to protect mankind from the pain and suffering caused by evil forces? And that—realizing this and all— they send their divine powers in the form of a woman?"

"Verily, you would be wise to consider the possibility that your mission might fail to be anything more than a footnote in history, were it not for the presence and assistance of Maa Durga, who manifests in many forms and is called by many names, the mother goddess who travels to the ends of the earth to protect her children from wickedness. She fills those who revere her with divine inspiration and a clever resourcefulness that leads to victory."

Orion couldn't help thinking that Joycelyn Eberhard was indeed actively engaged in helping the country's schoolchildren, abating the evils of ignorance, poverty, and inequality in the remote Sherpa village of Khumjung when this epic journey first began, while he was, well, simply running for the sake of running.

"You need to consider the possibility that one or all of you—this very day—might be the instruments of Durga Bhagwati's divine inspiration."

"Did you hear that, Dahmer? We might be the instruments of divine inspiration!"

Dahmer, who had moved to the edge of their cover to get a better view of the movements across the gorge, slid back to the group. "I hear you clear enough … and so will the enemy if you don't pipe down and let the Gurkha finish his prayers."

"You need to realize that a temple is built as a palace in which the gods actually live. It is a sacred place unlike any other place on the earth. When you approach such a consecrated temple with your heart and your mind, you associate yourself with the deity in a very sensitive manner; you become conscious of the deity's divine presence. As you approach the sanctum sanctorum you become more fully aware that an intelligent being—greater and more resplendent than yourself—is there, safeguarding you, knowing your innermost thoughts, helping you to cope with and to prevail against even the most dicey and difficult situation. You become conscious and confident that your immediate needs are recognized in this inner spiritual realm."

"Can you believe it? I'm getting chills!" said LaFleche with an expression of amazement, suggesting he was truly more surprised than skeptical.

"You can feel the presence of the divine being as a radiation emanating from the beautiful, invincible Durga. Even her name issues forth the destruction of '*du*,' devils, '*r*,' diseases, and '*ga*,' sins of injustice, cruelty, and irreligion. The vibrations of divine force you feel are called *Shakti*, and these vibrations may be accompanied by a clairvoyant vision or a refined cognition received through the various *chakras* of your own nervous system. This is the way of the warrior goddess Durga Bhagwati."

"I can feel something too—that's for sure," said Dahmer. "My hands are actually shaking. But I reckon my anxiety has more to do with the number of camouflage outfits I see coming this way—which we're gonna have to deal with pronto—than any divine radiations coming from the temple fortress and that goddess of yours."

"You can sense that a subtle message has been received, though not always consciously, and this message from the Deva is manifest in your life as a communication more real than any language you know. *Shakti* from the radiant temple of the Deva can change the life of an individual; in a gradual and patient manner, it can alter the life currents within your body; it can draw your awareness into deeper levels; it can change the patterns of karma by clearing out obstacles and issues dating back many past lives."

From the cover of the ridge, Dahmer sighted his rifle directly across the gorge, counting the numbers of porters passing into the anticipated kill zone. "Looks to be about a dozen or more uniformed Maoists, and about twice that many porters."

"Let the lead parties pass on by," said LaFleche in a hushed voice. "We've got bigger problems coming up behind them, as far as I can tell." LaFleche handed Orion his field glasses and began to load additional magazines into the pockets of his jacket and cargo pants. "See if you can get a bead on their weaponry without being seen," he said to Dahmer.

"Roger that," said Dahmer, and he crawled to a more forward position and began to survey the long lines of armed men gradually coming into view from the south.

Orion's heart began to beat wildly as he glassed the cliffs across the gorge for any signs of Joycelyn and the schoolchildren; alas, to no avail. Espying the large number of uniformed soldiers in the distance, he suddenly realized that they would soon be fighting a losing battle. All the while, Segunda sat there smiling with a look of supreme confidence that defied all logic.

Dahmer crawled back to the covered position and reported that the main force was heavily armed with an impressive assortment of carbines and brand-new automatic weapons, which they had obviously absconded from the Royal Army during their raids on the government installations. "They appear to be better armed than we are," he said.

"If they manage to flank us, and I suppose they will," said LaFleche, "this little ambush of ours could turn out to be our last hurrah." He removed his cap and sunglasses and wiped the beads of sweat off his forehead with his sleeve. "Well, what do you think, men? Are we fearless instruments of divine inspiration, aided and abetted by a fierce demon-fighting Durga, or should we turn tail and live to fight another day?"

"There's no time to die like the present," said Dahmer, trembling with anticipation.

"I didn't come this far to turn back without even trying," said Orion. "I'm not sure what good I can do for us at this range, but you can count on me to stand to the end."

"Well, then it's settled," said LaFleche. "Give the smirking Gurkha a rifle, and let's get this show on the road."

As Orion and LaFleche crawled into a firing position to the left, Dahmer adjusted the stock of an M4A1 assault rifle, slapped in a magazine and handed it over to Segunda, who remained seated like a yogi. Then Dahmer moved out into a firing position off to the right and stared in amazement at what he saw coming down the trail across the canyon from the north.

The warrior poised at the moment of battle does not ask whether dreams of heaven and greatness should be waiting for him in his grave; rather, he treats each moment in the silent spectacle of the eternal present as if it were unique and urgent and imperative. With the deep reconnaissance patrol about to engage in a battle they couldn't possibly win, and with Segunda seemingly possessed by reflections of an old temple that scarcely existed, Dahmer suddenly *saw* something he hadn't noticed before, something he just couldn't resolve.

He scrambled back to Segunda and issued an animated interrogative: "Segunda, old boy ... how, exactly, did the goddess Durga Bhagwati dispatch that evil demon?" His facial expression was that of intense interest.

"As you come to know and love the deity that you experience within the temple of your mind, she extends her sublime psychic assistance, informing you that evil can be overcome in many constructive ways—some directly by direct action, others indirectly by indirect action. Her countenance is seen as immensely beautiful as well as brutal. In her multitude of hands are many different weapons; her gift to you comes with that bold resourcefulness which always leads to victory."

"The demon, Segunda! The demon!" shouted Dahmer in exasperation. "How did the beautiful goddess kill the terrible demon beast?"

"You already know the answer," said Segunda. "It is clear to you now, as though the goddess had placed the weapon directly in the palm of your hand. In her epic battle with the shape-shifter Mahishasura, who had unleashed a reign of terror upon the heavens and the earth, the goddess used a fair number of her weapons, as the demon was capable of changing at will into many primitive forms. You should recall that the last rendition of Mahishasura was that of the buffalo demon, which the Durga subsequently dispatched."

"That's it!" cried Dahmer, nearly beside himself with excitement.

"What the hell are you yelling about, Dahmer?" scolded LaFleche, who had returned back to the spot with Orion to sort out the commotion. "Have you lost your mind?"

"No, man, I've got the answer. I mean, I've got a really cool strategy."

"Well, spit it out, dammit!" roared LaFleche.

"We target the next yak caravan that is presently coming down through the gorge from the north."

"I repeat ... have you lost your mind? There is an army of Maoists moving on the cliffs right in front of us."

"No, man, I'm clear as a bell," said Dahmer. "You see, if we target the wild nature of the beast, we'll get the Maoists. In fact, if we precisely target the uncontrolled and predictably disruptive nature of the beast, we'll get lots and lots of the bad guys."

Suddenly, a smile appeared on each of the men's faces, which brightened appreciably as if a torch was simultaneously illuminated in the inner sanctums of their minds. Moreover, there appeared a distinctive wave of enthusiasm that spread through the group like the flow of electricity, and they each in turn appeared to beam, much like Segunda had been beaming all along, with a posture of supreme confidence.

Without further prompting, the men of the long range reconnaissance patrol gathered their gear and headed northward along the protected ridge, moving gingerly from cover to cover to avoid being exposed in plain view. The team moved rapidly in an effort to reposition themselves in relation to the main force of insurgents which were moving up along the opposite cliffs. Dahmer motioned for Orion to join him in the point position, virtually goading him with confidence: "You can hit the broad side of a buffalo, can't you?" said Dahmer, and the two men raced on up ahead.

When they reached the point of the yak caravan descending along the cliffs, Dahmer suddenly stopped and, panting rapidly for breath, began to readjust the optical sighting scope on his M4A1 carbine. Then he adjusted the sighting module and telescoping stock on Orion's assault rifle, which was equipped with the same SOPMOD (Special Operations Peculiar Modifications) package, and handed the weapon back to Orion. Dahmer nodded with obvious approval when Orion tapped in a magazine, turned the rifle on its side, and moved the safety lever to "SEMI" for single-shot functionality. Together they moved forward into a firing position, and then the marksmen drew beads on their targets: the rear flanks of the heavily laden yaks.

Two shots rang out and echoed up and down the gorge. One shot, presumably Orion's, blasted the rock cliff into dust and fragments just above the yak train. The other found its mark on the hindquarters of an unfortunate animal, which bellowed and stumbled back, yet remained standing, struggling to keep its footing on the declivitous trail. Nothing else happened. Two more shots rang out, and two yaks began to act strangely, one shedding white crystalline salt from a rupture in one of the colorful woolen bags that it carried, and the other charged awkwardly forward as if it had been struck in the buttocks by lightning. More shots rang out, and all hell began to break loose as the yak train rampaged forward in motion. Unable to pivot around on the narrow trail, the frightened beasts charged forth in a panic, barging clumsily along the cliff face, driving stalled yaks and startled yak herders violently off the ledge. The sights and sounds of men and beasts shrieking and flailing in the air, tumbling down, down, down to their deaths on the rocky cliffs exacerbated the immediate horror and intensified the panic of the herd.

Then all hell really broke loose when the first of the rampaging yaks reached the main troop of Maoists, who had been moving slowly up the trail but who now stood frozen with horror, pressed up against the cliff face like stationary targets in a shooting gallery. Some kneeled down in a defensive position, and others crowded to escape back the way they had come. More shots rang out in rapid fire; this time it was LaFleche and Segunda who were firing in short bursts, cutting down the retreating Maoists and closing the door on their escape. The uncontrolled strength of the linear stampede crashed and bludgeoned through the enemy lines, hurling the Maoists off the cliffs like so many rag dolls, filling the gorge with the echoing screams of their falling.

The carnage on the cliff face turned out to be as awe-inspiring as it was complete. Halting the fearsome progression of the Maoists was one thing, to be sure, but the manner in which the deadly carnage was made manifest—by unleashing the natural propensities of the ungovernable against the ruthless authorities of the unprincipled—was truly a thing of beauty, and a great success in military terms. With literally hundreds of uniformed Maoists eliminated, the main burden of the trailing enemy force was virtually eradicated, leaving only the lead parties of insurgents, who had managed to pass by the ill-fated yak caravan, to contend with in the days to come.

The men of the deep reconnaissance patrol moved on in silence. They followed the river north for days, winding their way through the canyon, which gradually widened into a fertile valley. They tracked high, keeping well above the terraced farmlands and the primitive water-driven flour mills, which appeared to be deserted, and yet the repetitive creaks of a stone grinding wheel could be heard above the splashing waters—it sounded like a dull needle stuck in the groove of an old phonograph record, endlessly repeating the idiosyncratic grind of the millstone, endlessly abrading the abandoned grist of the reapers' harvest to dust. They steered clear of a small settlement where the grim remains of a former police station were still smoldering in the foreground. It was clear that the Maoist insurgents had moved out in a hurry, for there was no one left among the living, no one to even think about burying the dead.

They climbed steadily on a trail surrounded by tall pine, fragrant juniper, and flaming red rhododendrons until the forest gave way to a series of alpine meadows and steep ridges high above the timberline. They moved up along these ridges on a series of lesser-used trails, working hard and struggling with the altitude, until they approached the crest of a high mountain peak. There, at the top of the pass, they stopped to reconnoiter and to survey the great expanse of the Himalayas that loomed up on the horizons, but mostly they stopped to reflect upon the stunning beauty of the unearthly panorama at hand— the emerald lushness of the thickly forested hillsides, the immense grandeur of the snow-capped mountains, the ethereal splendor of the encompassing clouds, and the cerulean blueness of the sky above were all reflected in the flawless mirror of the Rara Tal, which shone brilliantly before them—it was as though they were each looking at the world from a place beyond our world, as though the lake itself was a picture window wherein everything that is, and was, and ever will be, was reflected perfectly in its waters.

9. Be Not Fond of the Dull Smoke-Colored Light

The inspired shooters of the long range reconnaissance patrol worked their way down the exposed slope of a grassy meadow fringed by layers of white birch trees and fragrant cypress, catching glimpses of wild Himalayan tahr maneuvering skillfully on the rocky ledges. Dropping down onto a trail that led into a dense forest of blue pine and black juniper, the men spotted an occasional musk deer on the run. They proceeded with caution; judging from the large number of fresh footprints on the trail, they knew they might encounter another sizeable force of enemy insurgents at any time. They followed the freshly trodden trail upstream in the general direction of the mirror lake until a rickety wooden footbridge came into view—it was badly weathered and gray with age—and they stopped abruptly to witness a most remarkable occurrence at the old gray bridge.

The bridge was occupied by a cluster of three local women wearing long, pleated skirts girded by simple cloth belts; their heads were covered with woven shawls that draped far down their backs; the fronts of their drab tunics were adorned by layers of colorful beads of various sizes and large amulets which hung around their necks. In addition to the three women on the bridge, there was a man transporting an impressively large burden on his back, the weight of which was carried up and over his shoulders by means of a thick strap that ran across the top of his head. It soon became clear that the burden he carried was the full weight of an apparently sickly old woman who was wrapped tightly in a woolen blanket, with only the extreme suffering of her woebegone face still showing.

The men of the reconnaissance patrol watched in awe and wonder as the porter approached the center of the bridge, where he stopped to enable the women to unwrap the woolen blanket and carefully unbind the old woman's legs, which then extended down and out at an angle. Holding tightly to one of the weathered pylons that supported the river-spanning wooden structure, the porter stooped to allow a portion of the weight of the old woman to be supported by the extension of her feeble legs against the crude planking of the bridge. It looked from a distance that the sickly old woman was holding onto what appeared to be a human baby or a doll the approximate size of a newborn infant.

If the villagers had spotted the men of the deep reconnaissance patrol—who had moved off the trail to avoid detection—they made no sign of it. There was only the seriousness of the occasion and the hush of the dense forest and the constant splashing of the headwaters that were flowing slowly through a marsh of reeds and under the planks of the bridge before escaping in a chorus of hushed whispers into the downward flow of the rocky stream. Suddenly, the old woman let out a high-pitched yawp and hurled the baby off the bridge into the obscurity of the dark waters. The three women watched as the mysterious object passed slowly beneath the bridge and disappeared with the splashing waters, falling headlong down into the stream. Then the porter stood upright; the women bound the old woman's legs against her chest, covered her again with the woolen blanket, and the villagers exited the scene, passing by the men of the long range reconnaissance patrol in a silent procession that acknowledged nothing at all.

Once the strange procession had vanished into the forest behind them, the men of the deep reconnaissance patrol looked to Segunda for an explanation, which was not immediately forthcoming. The pregnant pause extended into the ever-present tense.

"These moments of strange occurrence at this old gray bridge belong to another period of time. The overwrought excitement of the previous day has already vanished among the shadows of the past; the dramas of tomorrow have not yet emerged from the future. You have found an intermediate space, where the routine business of life does not intrude, where the passing moment of curiosity lingers and becomes truly the present. You have found a place to pause by the side of the road, a spot where Old Father Time, when he thinks that no one is watching him, sits down by the wayside to take a breath. Oh that he would fall asleep and let us mortals live on without growing old or ill."

The other men looked on in silence, keeping perfectly still, lest the slightest motion dissipate the intensity of the predilection.

"Now, being irrevocably awake, you peer through the half-drawn curtains of this earthly amphitheater only to observe the darkening world around you as a frozen dream. The snow-covered mountain peaks of the distant scenery ascend like white spires which direct you to the wintry luster of the firmament. Such a cold and forbidding skyline with the distant water all hardened into rock; such a frosty sky that it might make you shiver, even though you are tucked inside the warmth of a thick woolen blanket and carried effortlessly aloft. You sink down and muffle your head in the blanket, shivering all the while, but less from the chill of your body than the chilling idea of a polar atmosphere where the dying and the dead are lying in their ice-cold shrouds and narrow coffins. You cannot persuade yourself that they neither shriek nor shiver when the snow is drifting upon them and the bitter blast is howling against the door of the tomb."

Such gloomy thoughts collected and settled upon the stilled members of the task force, casting a somber complexion over this wakeful hour.

"In the depths of every heart there is a tomb and a sarcophagus, though the lights and commotion above may cause us temporarily to forget their existence. At a time like this, when the mind is dreadfully uncertain and the imagination is a mirror imparting vividness to all ideas, without the power of selecting or controlling the composition, you would just as soon make an examination of your own image of perfection and project it optically into the boundless sky. Rather that, than have the dark receptacles of death flung open wide; rather that, than have the funeral train come gliding by on cold, steely tracks upon which fear and doubt assume bodily shape and the fearsome objects of the mind become dire specters to the eye."

Orion tried hard to keep the morbidity of his dark forebodings from rising to the surface. But it was too late for that! There emerged among the earliest shades of his sorrow a pale mourner wearing a faint likeness to his true love, sadly beautiful with a hallowed sweetness in her lovely features and a gracefulness in the flow of her satin gown. Next, there appeared a shade of ruined loveliness, with dust among her golden tresses, her crimson garments all faded and defaced. Orion averted his glance from the view of the other men, his head drooping with disappointment and his heart nearly bereft of hope, for there emerged a harsher form of fatality in his mind—one with a stern brow of wrinkles that looked right through him with adamantine authority and great, lifeless eyes while pointing a long gray finger in his direction, attempting to touch that sore place in his heart.

Segunda must have sensed the tragic influence his dramatic preamble was having on the uninitiated in his charge, and so he hastened to complete his commentaries on the event they had presently witnessed with a more tangible explanation of the religious context of the setting and the medicinal purpose of the esoteric ritual involved.

"You are entering the remote lands of the Mugu and Humla districts, where elements of Masta animism are fused with orthodox Hindu beliefs, where the Bhotias of Tibetan origin have trickled south from the Asiatic steppes, melding the ancient Bonpo shamanism with steady waves of Tibetan Buddhist practice, forming a colorful tapestry of supernatural beings and powers wherein the local deities and demons are collectively interwoven into a fabric of folk medicine and practice that is more about ritual and custom than the subtleties of either scientific or theological understandings."

Segunda was still talking when the patrol approached the first pylons of the bridge.

"Now that you have witnessed an exercise in *the natural liberation of fear through the ritual deception of death*, you can each compose your own effigy in your own human form, and you can throw them into the maw of the river, shouting, *Take them! Take them! Oh mighty malignant ones! Your cravings! Your attachments! Your clinging! Your grasping! Your most fearful thoughts!*" Segunda led the patrol out onto the bridge, and he swung his arms sideways in the same manner as the sickly old woman. "*Let go of them!*" he shouted. "*Let go of them and be free!*"

Dahmer and LaFleche followed Segunda across the bridge, each mimicking the high-pitched yawp of the old woman as they mimicked the gesture and bounded across the bridge. Orion, on the other hand, crossed the bridge in silence, for he simply could not bring himself to ignore the reality of the foreshadowing that crept across his mind.

————————

Tired and hungry, the men made camp in the forest above the lake. A thorough search in their packs confirmed that there were no more military MREs among them. Fearing that they might be in close proximity to the enemy, they avoided an open fire, opting instead to utilize Orion's camp stove to heat what odds and ends remained of their dehydrated foodstuffs combined into a thin and motley stew. For dessert, they passed around the last of the stale crackers decked out with the dregs of the peanut butter and the cheese spread, each man taking a small, proportional bite of the meager ration before passing it on to the next guy. They sat together in silence, listening for the telltale sounds of human activities far off in the distance and watching the waxing moon through a break in the trees as it rose ever so slowly over the distant summits, casting an illusory image of its own reflection across the somber waters of the lake. At the far northern reaches of the lake, there appeared smaller reflections of distant campfires.

At daybreak, the men moved out along a damp trail, wading

through dewy grass and wildflowers and ushering a flush of crested grebes out from the shoreline onto the crystal-clear waters of the lake. An early morning fog obscured all but the immediate surroundings, and the elegant grebes soon disappeared into the mist. At the northernmost reaches of the lake, the men came across a macabre scene where a band of Maoist guerrillas had obviously camped for the night, dining on prime cuts from a number of indecorously butchered yearling sheep whose wooly carcasses were heaped and rotting on the exact spots where they had been slaughtered. The ashes from the campfires at the lakeside campsite were still warm, and yet the charred, half-eaten remains of the severed legs and shoulders of the lambs were presently attracting flies. Such waste would have been incomprehensible for a local herder, thought Orion as he passed by the ogre's carnage. Dahmer looked to be particularly disgusted, for he had covered his nose and mouth with the raised neckline of his Eminem T-shirt. Up ahead, Segunda and LaFleche were carefully estimating the number of the enemy insurgents—which they figured to be about sixteen—from the fresh compressions of the surrounding grasses.

Following the conspicuous trail of the ill-mannered insurgency, the patrol climbed a broad ridge of conifers and rhododendrons before dropping into the desolate valley of the Mugu Karnali River. There were no Maoists, porters, traders, or even local villagers on the rocky trail before them, only a vast mountain wilderness of paths to be transited on foot and a river to be crossed over by means of a far-flung suspension bridge—which Dahmer summarily unhinged with two well-placed explosive charges.

Climbing steadily from the former suspension bridge crossing, the patrol toiled upward for much of the day without food, sparing the little potable water they carried. The trail led them up and up through the rocky landscape to a high ridge, where they passed over the mountain on an exposed grassy knoll and on into the spectacular Humla Karnali Valley, where the forested slopes gave way to the pale cliffs of Humla, and the pale cliffs gave way in turn to the jagged peaks and magnificent skyline of the high Himalayas—a skyline dominated by the glowing snow-capped mountains of the Saipal Himal and the great soaring ridges of the Gurla Mandhata massif that loomed across the border in Tibet.

Step by step, the men of the long range reconnaissance patrol grew nearer to the militia they were tracking. With each new challenge, demanding intense concentration and inordinate personal commitment to the covert operation, the close-knit unit was becoming ever more suited for deep penetration into the extreme environs of these elusive, far-off battlegrounds in their arduous quest for that illusive Beauty, of whatever kind, which invariably excites the human soul to tears and other extremities. Such *Beauty is a terrible and awful thing*, as Dostoyevsky once noted. It is terrible because Beauty has not been nor can ever be fathomed; it is an enigma, a mystery that weighs men down to earth; it is an ideal that sets the mind on fire, as in days of youth and innocence, and yet this fathomless ideal exists in a territory that is fraught with both contradiction and delusion. Indeed, true Beauty appertains to that place where the gods and the demons are forever fighting, a bloody awful battlefield that is the beating heart of man.

Transiting ridge after ridge amidst an increasingly arid terrain, the men made their way along a series of deep valleys and ravines, where turquoise rivers slowly snaked through broad basins or suddenly churned with a distinctive hiss into milky rapids that disappeared from view with the serpentine twists and turns of the canyons. The trekking was arduous, to be sure, and they were physically running on empty, but the men were unified in purpose by the sheer intensity of their quest. An aerie of eagles soared silently, watchfully overhead as the long range reconnaissance patrol grew nearer to its goal.

They were descending down a precipitous slope into a broad valley, approaching the confluence of the thundering Humla Karnali River, when Segunda signaled for everyone to FREEZE with the motion of his fist raised to the level of his head. Without removing his pack, he signaled ENEMY IN SIGHT by hoisting an imaginary rifle to shoulder level and pointing said rifle in the direction of what looked to be a cluster of mediaeval houses arrayed along a level ledge carved into the steep hillside. Backing up slowly from his point position, Segunda turned to face the others—who had all stopped in their tracks—and extended his arm up at an angle from horizontal, palm down, and then lowered it rapidly to his side. While Orion was not fully trained in the nuances of military hand signals, he could recognize the international symbol for TAKE COVER well enough, and he did so without further prompting.

The thundering torrents of the Humla Karnali made it difficult for Orion to hear himself think, let alone to communicate with the others. Nevertheless, in anticipation of the likelihood of direct action, and in lieu of any particular instructions, each member of the long range reconnaissance patrol began to unpack and assemble the assault weapons that they carried in their expedition packs. Before the men had a chance to group up and plan a proper strategy, Segunda approached LaFleche—who handed him his field glasses—and together they crept forward to survey the situation at hand. Dahmer and Orion crawled up behind them, maintaining cover, yet watching carefully for each and every new insight.

Segunda held up the binoculars and glassed the scene below. LaFleche signaled for Dahmer and Orion to traverse farther to the right, which they did by means of a modified leopard crawl, carrying their weapons in their hands as they advanced in low silhouette. Straining to see the village down below without being seen, Orion could scarcely make out the gist of what amounted to a strange and chaotic sight. First, there was a bizarre assemblage of extravagantly attired humanoids wearing swags of fur and colorful gowns and fantastic nightmarish masks. And these carnival-like performers were leaping and spinning around wildly, as if possessed, brandishing long upraised staffs. Next, there were the approximately sixteen Maoists clad in their characteristic camouflage uniforms. In addition to the frenzied staff-wielding impersonators of the supernatural, there were clusters of excited villagers that were separate and distinct from the troop of uniformed Maoist insurgents in their midst. The periodic thumps of a drum and the eruptive clashes of cymbals could be discerned, but just barely, above the constant din of the surging river. From his distant vantage point, it appeared to Orion that the Maoists were not in possession of any of hostages but were in the process of harassing the irate carnival performers against the animated protests of the villagers, and that the frenzied staff-wielding impersonators of the supernatural were attempting to fend off the Maoists with their wild gyrations and the imaginary powers of their wooden sticks.

Perhaps, with the benefit of his field glasses, Segunda could see more clearly what was happening in the village down below. Perhaps there was some triggering event. Perhaps, in the heat of the chaos of the moment, there was some precipitous point of eventuality that leads a man from the ivory towers of contemplation and dispassionate observation to the point of dramatic action. All that is known for certain is the action itself—Segunda charged, all by himself, in a mad dash down the steep hillside, and the final words he shouted to his incredulous companions as he charged forth down the slope: "Time to risk a life! A Life!" he said. And then he was gone.

"Good god, cover the man!" barked LaFleche while readying his weapon.

Dahmer immediately rose to a kneeling position, shouldered his M4, and fired, taking out a startled Maoist as the Gurkha bounded toward the village with his H&K Mark-23 handgun in one hand and his unsheathed kukri knife in the other.

LaFleche steadied his M4 on the edge of a rock, squinted through the scope, and fired a single round from the prone position, taking down another uniformed insurgent. Several more shots rang out, and several more Maoists bit the dust before the insurgents realized what was happening. Orion began to panic, realizing that his limited expertise in sniping did not allow him to fire into a crowd with any certainty that he would be able to hit the target he was aiming at. Still, in all the chaos and confusion, he could see that Segunda would soon be the only feasible target for a dozen or so angry Maoists. He leapt up from his covered position and, avoiding a path that would take him into Dahmer's direct line of fire, tore down the rocky slope like a slalom ski racer, moving energetically from side to side and firing short bursts into the air as he went.

The outlandish maneuver created a unique moment of uncertainty, a moment of *tactical surprise and violence of action* which Dahmer and LaFleche took full advantage of, in terms of increasing the body count. The chaos and confusion escalated into a state of complete pandemonium when Segunda charged into the melee with his handgun blazing and his kukri knife slashing the enemy combatants to death with stunning quickness and precision. From the vantage point of a large rock outcropping just above the killing grounds, Orion witnessed firsthand the masterful proficiency of the Gurkha. By the time the others arrived at the scene, Segunda had dispatched the last remnants of the ill-fated insurgency, and he was busy collecting new specimens to add to his grisly scrolls, his Maoist scrolls of the *dead* and the *dreadfully deaf.*

Dahmer and LaFleche descended into the village burdened with the load of hastily discarded expedition packs, which were immediately relieved from their possession by the helping hands of a bevy of exceedingly thankful villagers. With his broad smile beaming approval, LaFleche thumped Orion on the back in a most amiable manner, stating, "At least this time you spared a few rounds for the rest of us." And when they all finished laughing, he added, "You may not know squat about military tactics, but you sure know how to make a spectacle of yourself."

More jocularity ensued. And then, Dahmer—who was desperately trying to catch his breath against the demands of the strenuous laughing—offered his opinion: "I think we finally found the one thing ... the one thing that Orion is actually good at!"

The triumphant men of the deep reconnaissance patrol were amazed to see that the majority of the villagers, along with what turned out to be an entire company of costumed Mani dancers (Bonpo demon-frightening shamans), had already formed a line and were in the process of removing the bodies of the Maoists from the village and carrying them off in the direction of the thundering green torrent of the Humla Karnali River.

When the villagers and the Mani dancers returned, an over-the-top outburst of impassioned emotion and affection was lavished upon the heroic members of the deep reconnaissance patrol-cum-hostage-rescue task force. The dramatic action relating to their timely and forceful arrival on the scene, taken together with deeply held beliefs in the *Supernatural Forces* that constituted the fundamental thematic essence and, thus, the primal purpose of the costumed Mani dancers, made an irresistible impression on every living soul within the village.

Through Segunda, Orion learned that the Mani Festival—which ordinarily celebrated the rites of spring in other, less wild-and-woolly environs—was an ongoing concern for these remote villages of the far, far west of Nepal, where life was harsh and death loomed ever-present, and where the conventional separations between men and women and the spirit world were reduced to nil. In these remote villages, the Mani performers were hardly a seasonal diversion but a long-established aspect of the ongoing religious ceremonies—ceremonies which pertained to the *constant* struggle against demons and their correlates in the evil behaviors of men.

Apparently, the Mani dancers served as a means by which the *Supernatural Forces* could be summoned outright and brought to bear against tenacious demons that had a tendency to kidnap local women and children. The theatrical performances were intended to transcend the mundane with the elaboration of rituals, traditional costumes, and sacred dances, which brought both deliverance and the protection of the gods that much closer to the world of man. In these isolated villages of Humla, where the infant mortality rate was atrociously high, where women and children routinely disappeared, where death and disease came like the fog, on not-so-little cat feet, the presence of the demonic was as easily seen as felt.

These villagers were characteristically devout, with their own unique and varied customs; yet, pragmatically fearing for the worst, they believed that the demons would surely return in the event that the village failed to perform the Mani rituals—specifically, the demons would return to take the lives of more of their women and children. It was in this theosophical context that the dramatic arrival of the men of the long range reconnaissance patrol was uniformly viewed as an auspicious occasion by the entire village, an occasion that called for the favorably inclined to bestow their favors upon these unlikely heroes with the unbridled enthusiasm of the redeemed.

In no time at all, the men were stripped of their western clothing, swabbed and bathed with herbal waters, and gowned with fresh textiles, goat skins, woven robes, and shawls in the manner of the Mani dancers which they now, in actuality, exemplified. Segunda was clad in an audacious rainbow tapestry with a white linen coiffure; LaFleche, in a sheepskin jacket turned inside out. A jubilant Dahmer sported a white shirt and a blue-dyed vest crossed with beaded bandoliers, which made him look like a garish pirate of another place and time. Orion was given black leggings and a bright red jacket that was girded by a hide belt onto which three silver bells were firmly affixed.

There was much discussion, haphazard translation, and general amusement in the selection of the various masks—which personified the extremes of human emotions, denuded skulls, clowns, fierce demons, protector deities, and/or animal faces—but there was no general agreement as to which mask or masks would be most befitting for each individual man, with the exception of Orion, where the selection of a wide-eyed innocent with an oversized bright yellow face bearing a somewhat surprised expression was thoughtfully selected. In no time at all, the men were stripped of their western identities and freshly arrayed in the most outrageous of disguises, shrouded inconspicuously among the arcane mysteries of local color and the inordinate theatricality of bad taste.

As twilight yielded to eventide, the aromas of food cooking over wood fires reminded Orion and his companions how truly hungry they had become. They literally salivated over the meal that was served to them in wooden bowls, albeit with great ceremony. In a land where subsistence farming was the rule and trading in Tibetan salt for lowland rice was a matter of necessity to make ends meet, the lavish spread of dried meat, buckwheat lakkad (pancakes), potatoes, and turnips seemed to them like a meal fit for a king; the presentation of cabbage, apples, and walnuts surpassed the culinary appeal of any Waldorf salad; the pulp of freshly harvested apricots seemed to their depleted palates to be the food of the gods. There was an abundance of fermented barley beer, which both Dahmer and LaFleche enjoyed in immodest quantities as the evening hours transported the celebration into the night.

And then there was the dancing, replete with triumphant reenacting of past and present cultural motifs, the relentless pounding of goat-skin drums, the rhythmic clangs of cowbells, and the scintillating clash of cymbals—it was an ever-blooming celebration in which the entire village was transformed into a theatrical stage, a stage upon which each and every member of the village was an active and integral performer. It soon became clear that the women of this village were imbued with a remarkable degree of sexual freedom. Dancing with abandon to the clamor of the exotic music, the equally exotic women of the village worked their own form of magic, bewildering the four FNG masqueraders, who were now bending and leaping upward in unison with the other costumed performers, twisting and gyrating provocatively and pointing their all-powerful prop-staffs skywards into thin air.

The unabashed flirtation intensified through the night as the theatrical stage itself extended from the village grounds up onto the interconnected decks of the flat rooftops, where strange and anonymous couples could be seen moving rhythmically in the shadows. After dancing a while longer, Orion looked around for his friends and his guide, only to realize that he was indeed the last man standing. If it remains true, as Natalie Clifford Barney once wrote, that *virtue is a demand for greater seduction*, then that would explain the renewed vigor and persistence by which the lingering, amazingly beautiful women of this long-suffering village were attempting to seduce Orion; for not only was he in the possession of impressive good looks and was therefore exceedingly attractive to the ladies, Orion was by nature inexorably chaste, having set his aching heart, his unsophisticated mind, and his innermost desire on that elusive Überjoy who remained, it seemed, above and beyond his reach. And although there were many desirable women who plied the feminine art of seduction long into the night, Orion could neither be the unleashed bow, the flaming arrow, nor the ultimate target of their womanly desires.

Nature itself hath no greater glory than the radiant ambiance of a suffering soul and/or an entire village that has been freshly exorcised of its demons. There is a delightful character of the smile that emanates unspoken appreciation, an ethereal leavening of the human spirit that coincides with a deepened sense of gratitude, a calmness and confidence of composure that reveals a newfound equanimity.

And then there was the look of Dahmer, Segunda, and LaFleche the next morning—it was an undeniable look of three cool cats who had just had their fill of canaries. Nonetheless, it was hard to leave this peacefully sleeping village at daybreak. And it was harder still to convince the troop of Mani dancers to hasten along with them to the anticipated rendezvous point up at Simikot. Thankfully, Segunda was able to convince the leader of the Mani troop to do just that, with the help of all of Orion's paper rupees and a few American dollars, which would buy a considerable amount of salt and/or rice and quite a few yaks in the bargain. Poverty, it seems, is an extremely effective motivator when it comes to recruiting.

The pace of the indigenous hikers in Nepal is generally an impressive thing to see, and these Humlis were no exception. It was all that the reconnaissance unit could do to keep up with their advanced guard, as it were, and it was generally Segunda who bridged the gap with the professional Mani dancers as the patrol spread out and made their way along the tortuous trails above the Humla Karnali. They moved through a series of lush green valleys with fragrant cedar forests, tracking high for expediency and to avoid unnecessary encounters with roving Maoists. The hiking was so hard and steep in places as to preclude the use of pack animals from the village.

The men of the deep reconnaissance patrol maintained their costumed disguises over their standard hiking clothes, and they managed to cover the exposed fabric of their store-bought expedition packs by lashing the curved half of a porter's woven basket onto the hip and shoulder straps of their gear. From time to time, they passed by locals threshing grain or spinning wool deftly by hand; only this time, the local villagers did not shrink back and disappear from view into obscurity, but they waved with both hands in salutation before pressing their palms together and bowing in a cordial gesture of *Namaste*.

The weather was mild and clear, and they made good progress till the end of the day, when the high clouds that wreathed the silhouetted peaks of Mount Api and Saipal turned to gold, and then to crimson, against a darkening purple sky. They grouped up with the lead party of Mani performers at the entrance of a fair-sized settlement. This was done for two reasons: the first being the dramatic necessity of a formal procession into the village, conducted in a manner befitting the august performance of a religious drama and/or a circus carnival; the second reason being the methodical assurance provided by the paramilitary players that the village would be physically cleared of any impious Maoists insurgents from the outset.

It turned out that this isolated settlement had indeed been recently set upon by the Maoist insurgency, which had extracted a heavy toll from the village in terms of taxes and provisions. Even worse was finding that several able-bodied children had been taken away, and that the Maoists had left a single shoe hanging in front of a number of the houses, indicating that these particular families were suspected to be hiding their children and that the Maoists would soon return to collect one child from each marked home to join their cause, lest the parents run the risk of becoming a tragic example. Under these conditions, it was abundantly clear that this village was definitely in need of some serious exorcising and that the protections offered by the traveling Mani dancers were welcomed most fervently, in much the same over-the-top manner as before.

Parading into the village with affectations of great pomp and circumstance, Orion experienced a brief moment of hesitation. "You guys aren't really planning to run amuck again with these lovely ladies, are you?"

Dahmer and LaFleche simply looked at each other and burst out laughing. Even Segunda was smiling—that same catlike smile as before. Segunda was smiling, but he wasn't answering any questions.

The stagecraft of the celebration erupted into a bawdy drama as the dancers pranced around the communal areas of the village, frightening away real and imagined demons that afflict the human spirit, replacing sadness and dread with good humor, attacking insurmountable fear with outrageous pantomime, combating the incipient penetration of misfortune and mortality with the elevation of sensuality, laughter, and forgetting.

Dahmer and LaFleche excused themselves temporarily to make contact with Sergeant Bane in Simikot and/or Captain Umbrage, now in Kathmandu. When they returned to the festivities, Orion could immediately tell that LaFleche was no longer laughing, or even smiling, for that matter. It was as though a shroud of some inescapable responsibility had suddenly fallen over him, along with a stern reminder that there are other, darker forces of nature that are not so easily dispelled. Attempting to hide his obvious expression of concern, LaFleche covered his face with a mask of Mahakala, a protector deity, or *dharmapala*, who constantly fights against the serpent spirits called *nagas* and is an important protector of the faith.

"What's up with LaFleche?" asked Orion, grabbing hold of Dahmer's arm.

"Too soon to tell," he replied in muffled speech, talking through his Mani clown mask with its ridiculous yak-fur beard.

"Can you please be more specific!" continued Orion.

"Look, man, there's something going on in the area. That's all we know. The reports are pretty sketchy."

"Then why does LaFleche look so worried?"

"Look, man. It might be okay. You see, the bad guys with your package might be arrivin' right on schedule."

"Then why does LaFleche look so worried?" Orion repeated.

"The reports are coming in from more than one direction."

"And what does that mean?" demanded Orion, shaking the reluctant Mani clown with both hands.

"Let go of me, dude, or I'll bash you with my ugly stick." Dahmer shook himself loose, twirled the Mani staff around, and posed fiercely in the manner of a martial artist. Then he relaxed as he approached Orion and said, "Seriously, dude, we're on it … and we'll know more soon. Meanwhile, try and have some fun while the women are willing and the moon still shines."

Plentiful food and drink was followed by music and ceremonial dancing, as before; ceremonial dancing was followed by carousing with reckless abandon and extended seductions on the rooftops, as before. The major difference from the previous evening was that Dahmer rousted Orion from his sleep in the middle of the night with the words, "Wake up, dude. We had best get a move on."

Orion laced on his hiking boots in the dark and climbed down the carved log ladder to the ground where Dahmer, Segunda, and LaFleche were already waiting for him with their disguises and their expedition gear. With their xenon headlamps piercing the darkness and the plumes of their anxious breaths rising up into the chill of the night, the unified men of the deep reconnaissance patrol reminded Orion of a steam locomotive panting at the station.

"What's the word?" asked Orion.

"Sooner is better is the only thing you need to know for now," said LaFleche.

"What about the Mani dancers?"

"They'll catch up with us tomorrow. But I don't expect they'll be much good if push comes to shove in the morning."

Orion fastened his headlamp to his forehead, shouldered his expedition pack, and followed the others out of the village.

They strode as fast as they could in the enveloping darkness, switching their headlamps on, as needed, and off again when the moon was released from the shroud of clouds and they could make out the path ahead as a lustrous ribbon in the moonlight.

At dawn, LaFleche pulled out his radio. Orion slowed his pace, stopping just round the next bend to provide LaFleche with some semblance of privacy.

LaFleche tried the radio without the aid of the tree antenna, and it crackled to life.

With the static and the distance, Bane's words were garbled. But even so, the urgency and desperation in the man's voice was clear, and Orion could make out the words "sabotage" and "the bastards." From the sound of it, the news wasn't good.

"Roger that," said LaFleche. Then, after an indiscernible squawk from the radio, he said, "Repeat," and turned to deflect the wind—which was gusting strongly with slashes of rain—holding the precious radio set that much closer to his ear.

Waiting for LaFleche to finish, Orion pictured the battle-scarred, long-haired hippie of a special forces operator he'd somehow grown attached to from a distance—their sole lifeline of vital information—and he hoped that Sergeant Bane was all right.

"Sounds like someone spotted your beauty queen with her schoolchildren!" shouted LaFleche as he stowed the squad radio in his pack. "But I don't like the sound of it!" he added.

"What do you mean?" shouted Orion, immediately beside himself with worry.

LaFleche explained that Simikot was under attack from multiple directions, and that the Maoists were using innocent women and children as human shields, enabling them to advance and to sabotage the only serviceable airstrip in the region, cutting the settlement in half and isolating the government forces in a bad way.

"What about the women and children?" shouted Orion. "What are you not telling me?"

"I told you I don't like the sound of it!" barked LaFleche. "I don't like the tone of Bane's voice!"

"What does that mean ... *exactly*!" implored Orion.

"Knowing Bane, it means he's not gonna fire on the enemy!" LaFleche concluded, clapping Orion on the shoulder as he passed him.

The wind was still gusting strongly and the rain was driven in sheets when they labored up the muddy thousand-meter climb to the far-flung hamlet of Simikot. Seen through Orion's eyes, through his horror and his fear, what had become of the once-thriving mountain community was the foul and caliginous substance of nightmares. An awful pall of death loomed dreary and dripping upon the surrounding hillsides, filling the terraced farmlands with a torrent of thick mud and blood that mingled with heaven's own tears and streamed down in great clots to the river below. The rainclouds hung dark and low over the broad shelf of ruined land that once supported the village, and although it was well past the stroke of noon, there was a palpable shadow of lurid smoke and a darkness that moved upon this nightmare landscape; it was a shadow of smoke and darkness that eclipsed the sun as it stifled the breath and chilled the hearts of the living. Yet there was no one left there among the living; there was only the dying and the dead.

As they approached what was left of the village, the men could see the charred remains of an army helicopter that was partially exploded from within and the smoldering hulk of a small, twin-engine airplane that had failed to ascend and escape and was flipped on its side in a ditch beside the runway with a wing broken off and all its windows shattered. Everywhere they looked, there were bodies lying on the rain-soaked ground. There were bodies of villagers and their children lying in the mud on the unpaved runway, and beyond the runway, at the entrance to the government compounds, there were bodies of villagers caught up in the wires and the barricades. Beyond the wires and barricades, there were the bodies of uniformed soldiers arrayed as they died in protective formations.

They found Sherpa Outré stripped of his clothes and much of his skin—it was apparent that both of his legs had been broken at the shins. Beside Outré lay the remains of a man whose upper body and face had been badly disfigured by some kind of explosion. The jacket had been stripped off the body, leaving the lifeless arms bare beyond the sleeves of a Hard Rock T-shirt and exposed to the pouring rain. "That's Q. T. Bane—may he rest in peace," said LaFleche in an uncharacteristic moment of sincerity. "I can recognize those battle scars he carried." LaFleche raised his hand in a brave salute to the fallen military men, and then he pivoted around sharply in the pooling mud and walked away with his face turned up into the rain.

Orion was initially stunned by the appalling carnage; however, he surely realized the vast implications of this momentous disaster, and he began to search haphazardly for his own recognizable *person of interest* in this ghastly village of the dead. Frantically, he turned over body after body, staring into the vacant faces of women and children, all of whom had perished far too young. His feelings of panic were transmogrified into a blinding fury when he realized how many of these hapless women and children of the damnable human shield had been shot in the back by their kidnappers. Others had been blown to bits by the homemade socket bombs that were strapped around their necks and/or held in their tiny hands. Orion sprang from one horrific mound to another in an ever-expanding circle of woe. He rambled and lurched about the killing fields like a madman, and he dug through the slippery blood and the muck of human ash and grease, searching for a glimpse or even a shred of something that was familiar and dear to him, hoping against hope in a half-crazed delirium and yet knowing all the while that he would rather tear the pounding heart from his own chest than find what he was looking for.

In his furious search beyond the compounds, Orion stumbled across a wounded Maoist soldier who had been left for dead but was not quite there. The injured insurgent was struggling to breathe with a sucking chest wound that was visible through a large hole in his camouflage uniform. At any other time in his life, Orion would have immediately rendered first aid, at the very least, as he was apt and well-trained to do. But not on this day, in this place, at this time—not in this nightmarish quagmire of horror and gore where fury and rage reigned supreme—he was desperate and demented, enraged and insane, and now, facing this enemy, he was caught up in arms with the devil himself. Orion grasped a large rock and pulled it savagely up from the muck, holding it high over his head in a wild and murderous pose, with every rabid intention of bashing the stricken man's brains in ... when he felt the wrath of his trembling arm stilled by the steady restraint of another.

It was Segunda who was kneeling in the mud right beside him. "Be not fond of the dull smoke-colored light from hell," he said in a calm, abiding voice. "You would soon become lost when you fall into these negative realms, sinking into a swamp of unbearable suffering from which there could be no escape. You would join the ranks of those anguished spirits that roam the world like hungry ghosts whose unquenchable appetites and thirst for vengeance leaves them powerless to fulfill or resist, for they are compelled to enter a land of darkness with deep earthen pits and black roads that lead to nowhere."

Segunda took the rock from Orion's hand and continued. "You, my starry-eyed companion, were born to a higher realm, a realm with a higher calling and purpose. You should always be mindful of your rightful disposition on this path. If and when you succeed in your mission, it will be for the benefit of many of those who are not yet born. It is a sublime purpose that will bring happiness to all living beings. And you will find that mighty forces will continue to come to your aid, to guide you and to help you accomplish this purpose. It is not for the likes of you to concern yourself with either conquest or vengeance."

With that, Segunda dispatched the unfortunate insurgent with a flash of his kukri knife and promptly collected his ears.

10. A Flock of Ladies on the Lake

A murder of crows issued harsh and haunting refrains that followed the men of the deep reconnaissance patrol out beyond the sodden plateau of the ruined village and across a patchwork of trampled-down fields. The echoing cries were accompanied by a silent sorrow that mounted up through the gloom and the rain; it hunched over the listless scene amidst the coverlet of rainclouds, looming large and unseen but not unnoticed. The men slogged up and over a meandering ridgeline and then down the slippery slopes of the forested landscape on a steep zigzagging trail that led into the vast basin of the seething Humla Karnali.

Following the course of the river upstream, they met up with the lagging troop of Mani performers, who seemed to sense the need to move quickly through this perilous place and time. The attacking Maoists and their droves of human shields appeared to have vanished into the dripping landscape. What remained was only the dull and dreary obligation of the pallbearer; it was an obligation that went unclaimed.

The coterie of nouveau Manis trekked with the accomplished players across steep sections of the river valley where the trails ran high above the roiling waters, narrowing at times to a mere wooden crosswalk that was supported by a dubious series of poles. Other sections of the trail were washed out entirely by small but significant landslides that continued to creep downhill. The company used their Mani staffs to probe and pick their way gingerly across these waterlogged inclines while the shedding rain from the blackest of clouds continued to bear down upon them.

They came across the bespattering spectacle of a waterfall, where they refilled their water bottles and rinsed the muck from their faces and hands, not bothering to remove either their waterproof packs nor the outer garments of their strange native clothing, for they were already soaked to the skin. The extended troop of Mani performers continued on through the deluge as though the torrential downpour was only a minor inconvenience. They passed several small settlements in which no one alive was seen to be moving; there was only the flutter of an occasional chicken that had escaped predation and the distinctive flapping of rain-soaked prayer flags that languished to the will of the wind.

Up and down they climbed through a progression of green gorges, negotiating treacherous sections with great care or climbing higher up to avoid otherwise impassible spans. They worked their way across the raging waters of a forested tributary valley and then climbed away from the main river to the crest of a ridge above the layer of low-lying clouds which had previously obscured their views of the Saipal Himal to the west. With the clearing of the inclement weather, they caught sight of a train of villagers with heavily burdened ponies descending down into the valley ahead of them, and just beyond the guided train of ponies, they saw a long line of men in telltale camouflage uniforms.

LaFleche moved up fast to the front and gave a signal for the lead Mani performers to stop; and then, without speaking to anyone, he reached into his pack and held up a magazine for the Mark-23 handgun, which he proceeded to stuff, among several other full clips, into his pockets; and then, without looking back, he raised the H&K Mark-23 OHWS (Offensive Handgun Weapon System) upward with its sound suppressor and its under-mounted laser module pointing to the sky. He made a distinctive circular motion in the air and then flicked the barrel in a forward direction, signaling the other members of the patrol to follow him onward. But before anyone else could respond to these hand signals, LaFleche was already moving double-time in the direction of the insurgents, leaving his pack and his fellow reconnaissance patrollers behind. By the time the others were able to move out in support, LaFleche had already worked his way past the caravan of startled villagers and heedless pack animals and was starting to engage the enemy.

Moving fast behind Dahmer and Segunda, Orion struggled to see what was happening. Racing by the stalled line of local rustics and big-headed ponies that were laden with oversized rolls and packs, Orion could make out the singular figure of LaFleche walking forward with the unwavering resolve of a Western gunfighter, stepping over a lineage of horizontal bodies of dead men that had been too slow to respond to the unanticipated directness of his assault. LaFleche continued to walk calmly and resolutely forward, reloading fresh clips in the blink of an eye while issuing a distinctive .45-caliber reprimand against any and all complaints. One by one, the formation of surprised Maoist insurgents turned to face LaFleche, to lurch backward, to duck for cover, or to ready their individual weapons—and one by one they fell. When the last of the long line of ill-fated insurgents slumped down into the mud, there was a cold and bitter wind that swept through the valley like some gigantic exhalation, and then there was quiet.

Finally, LaFleche slid the handgun into the belt of his pants and turned back around. Though silent still, the bleakness of his unsmiling expression spoke loud and clear—it spoke of the unbreakable bond between brothers in arms; it spoke of the inconsolable remorse of having arrived too late; it spoke of the unbearable loss of a fallen field commander; in other words, it spoke in silent memoriam for Sergeant Q. T. Bane.

The baffled porters were happy to have their pack animals appropriated by this curiously subdued yet astonishingly efficient member of the of traveling Mani performers, who was able to expurgate the entire valley of its nefarious offensiveness without so much as breaking stride. They were happier still when Segunda paid them handsomely—with Orion's remaining American dollars—for six of the sturdy ponies, sending the locals back to their villages with an abundance of replenishments and a marvelous story to tell.

The deep reconnaissance patrol continued on at a good pace, with the weight of their packs and provisions distributed on the sure-footed ponies and the abiding light-hearted mirth of the Mani performers briskly leading the way. They maintained a high route on a solid trail for the benefit of the pack animals, moving away from the Humla Karnali, which soon disappeared around the bend of a steep and seemingly impassable gorge. Darkness overtook them on a long uphill pull, and they made camp in a broad, grassy clearing with good water for the men and the beasts.

Dahmer set up a tree antenna, and LaFleche managed to make contact with Captain Umbrage on the squad radio. By the sound of the abbreviated conversation, Captain Umbrage was duly informed of the debacle up at Simikot and the deaths of all the allied forces, and yet the abrupt disconnect that followed—without any signing off—indicated that LaFleche was not about to entertain any new ideas about aborting the mission or returning to any Nepalese army bases without getting the job done. This realization filled Orion with a profound sense of relief and—although he did not quite understand it—he felt a strong bond of solidarity with his acutely determined colleagues. There would be no disagreement found among this unlikely band of brothers; from this day to the ending of the world, it would be remembered that there was simply *no quit* in them.

Gathering around the warmth of a campfire to dry out their socks and clothing, LaFleche finally opened up to the others.

"What we've got here, men, is a purposeful failure to communicate," he said with a theatrical Southern drawl reminiscent of an old movie. His eyes gleamed brightly with the reflected light of the campfire.

Orion nodded in tacit approval, his own eyes squinting into the flames, his mind cut off from his suffering heart as though the two were separated by a mountain of stones.

"What we once had as a long range reconnaissance patrol was

a covert operation, or black op, for you novices," said LaFleche, looking directly at Orion, who suddenly nodded to attention.

"Roger that," said Orion.

"A covert operation," continued LaFleche, "is an operation that is planned and authorized and executed in such a manner as to permit plausible deniability by the federal authorities."

"A covert operation is designed to conceal the identity of the *sponsor*," added Dahmer, setting his wet socks out on two elevated sticks in the process.

"But those days are behind us," said LaFleche.

"And what, may I ask, is in front of us?" queried Orion, moving his unlaced hiking boots a little closer to the fire.

"What we have here is a clandestine operation," said LaFleche in the manner of a monk imparting some deep and contemplative metaphysical distinction.

"And that's not the exact same thing?" questioned Orion.

"No, it is not," said LaFleche.

"Not the same thing at all," agreed Dahmer, slowly shaking his head.

"You know, it's really not," confirmed Segunda.

"So what's the big secret?" responded Orion with mounting indignation.

"We're it ... the big secret ... if you really wanna know," blurted Dahmer.

"Are you guys joking, or is a clandestine operation a different kind of deal?"

"A clandestine operation is conducted in such a manner as to ensure complete secrecy and concealment of the entire operation," said LaFleche. Dahmer grinned with amusement as LaFleche continued. "A clandestine operation differs from a covert operation in that the emphasis is placed on the concealment of the *operation itself* rather than concealment of the identity of the sponsor."

"Do ya get it, dude?" prompted Dahmer, adjusting the elevation of his sock sticks.

"Yes, I think so," said Orion. He stood and reached over to the fire with a padded hand to retrieve a pot of boiling water. "But how does that change anything for us?"

"It changes everything," said LaFleche with a note of seriousness. "With Bane dead, we have no official sponsor or mission—covert or otherwise. And now that we have donned the clandestine attire and habit of these here Mani dancers," he said, motioning to the Manis who had set up their own camp and cook fire a few hundred feet away, "we are entirely off the grid."

"You had best believe that no one is even going to think about coming to your rescue, should things turn out badly," said Segunda in a surprising outburst of explanatory rhetoric. "You need to realize, from here on out, that you are entirely on your own."

"Right you are, Segunda. And if anyone would know what it's like to be a man with a mission and a man without a country at the same time, it would be a Gurkha."

"So, beside that fact that we are traveling off the grid to the far side of the moon, is there anything that we are planning to do differently from here on out?" asked Orion.

"From here on out, Orion, we are in this thing so deep that the only auspices we have going for us is our own resourcefulness and our stealth."

Black sleep came easy to the men of the clandestine operation, while frost came hard to all the exposed surfaces of the campground. At daybreak, they packed up the ponies and headed into the frosted expanse of wilderness with cautious optimism that they were hot on the trail of Joycelyn Eberhard and her kidnapped schoolchildren. They traveled the better part of two days on rocky trails, rising up in altitude into evergreen forests and along precipitous outcroppings with clear views of the empty trails ahead.

At one point, they came across a ragtag group of young Nepali men and women who appeared disheveled and confused but uninjured, having somehow managed to elude their handlers or captors and were attempting to make their way back to their home villages. The men and women clapped as they ran toward the lead party of Mani performers, and Segunda was able to ascertain that a sizeable band of Maoists—with what appeared be hostages—was indeed headed for the border with the fear that there was some kind of Royal mega force in pursuit. Little did these returning villagers know that the fearsome mega force was, in actuality, the friendly troop of masked Mani dancers who had just given them food and fresh provisions before sending them on their way.

They struggled with the ponies up a stiff and relentless climb to the Nara Lagna pass, where the ground turned from dirt to snow and ice and the trail led them higher to the level of the nearby clouds. The great snowcapped mountains to the southwest were wreathed with a layer of these light, sinuous vapors, while the imposing white bulk of the Gurla Mandhata massif loomed straight ahead, rising unadorned into the clear blue skies of Tibet. The crest of the pass was marked by a large heap of stones and a prodigious collection of prayer flags that were badly faded and tattered by the wind, their auspicious symbols, thoughtful inscriptions, invocations, mantras, and prayers having been progressively disseminated by nature for the benefit of all sentient beings. Among the traditional prayer flags was a diverse assortment of windblown silken scarves, often used as a sign of devotion, a personal recognition of one's love and respect for another. Several of the authentic Mani performers stopped and affixed a number of new flags to the streaming festoons to ensure good fortune and prosperity, and then they casually threw a few handfuls of roasted barley into the air before moving on with the ponies.

Orion lingered at the spot for quite some time, watching the colorful chorus of flags flapping wildly in the wind. He sat there panting at the base of the stone cairn while the others moved on ahead. Crushed by the weight of his emotions, Orion struggled to hold onto the glimmer of light and a hope that was rapidly fading from his heart, suffering with all the anguish of a childish love that had been cast by wretched disillusionment into a stone-cold dungeon of despair that created its own darkness within. Right then, right there, upon that great chaotic heap of rubble and flags that are exposed to the harshest of elements, Orion left something of himself behind—be it the last satin threads of the optimism he carried, the crowning crimson blush of his ardent heart's desire, or the finally fading shred of his own innocence—it was placed there in silence and left wafting in the high mountain breezes as some form of prayer. And then Orion moved on quickly to catch up with the others.

Once the caravan of Mani dancers and ponies that comprised the clandestine operation had crossed over the treacherous ice fields of the high mountain pass, they could see the great fluted walls of a broad, treeless valley spreading out before them in all the mineral colors of ocher; they could follow the meandering contours of the Humla Karnali that had returned to the landscape and was now carving its way through the center of this valley; they could make out the thin paired cables of a widespread suspension bridge that started out in Nepal and ended its river crossing in China.

From the crest of the pass, at 15,900 feet, the procession descended down nearly 4,000 feet in altitude on a dizzying sequence of switchbacks through barren boulder-strewn slopes which were flanked by an abundance of loose talus scree and steep, unprotected drops. It was nearing midday by the time they made their way down the barren and exposed mountainsides and into a deserted village along a dusty track where small whitewashed houses stood empty with all the windows shuttered. Slipping and sliding at times on the unforgiving surfaces of sand and loose stones, the men and ponies finally arrived at the banks of the Humla Karnali, where they secured the more clandestine aspects of their loads before heading single file up the stone ramp and over the steel-cable suspension bridge of the unattended border, crossing virtually unnoticed into Tibet.

The caravan of Mani dancers and ponies made their way through the barren foothills to the outskirts of a Tibetan trading village, where they joined a large gathering of caravans that were going nowhere fast. There, among the slew of traders, were a number of yaks carrying huge building timbers and an even greater number of sheep and goats carrying small sacks of grain; however, they all appeared to be stalled by a larger assembly of porters and pack animals that were being unloaded of their burdens amid an unsettling assembly of traveling Indian businessmen and pilgrims, uniformed Nepalese Maoists, and a convoy of Chinese Army trucks. It didn't take long for everyone to realize that there was some kind of high-value trading going on at this very moment.

LaFleche made a series of discrete hand signals, moving his hand from his brow to his throat, and finally to the line of Chinese Army trucks. Dahmer nodded in affirmation and grabbed Orion's arm. "This is it," was all he said.

Orion's heart began to race as he realized how close he was at last.

Apparently and appallingly, in the midst of the seasonal market where spices and textiles and coffee and jewelry were sold or exchanged each year for sheep and grains and wool, there was yet another kind of transaction in the making, and it involved a prize of the two-legged kind. It was becoming clear that the Peace Corps volunteers and their kidnapped Nepalese schoolchildren were either held inside these canvas-covered vehicles or they had already been carted off. In any event, it was clear that a contingent of the People's Liberation Army was somehow involved in the transactions and that these army trucks were the key.

Orion felt like bolting forth. *But how? And where, precisely, to begin?* He looked over at the thinly disguised countenances of Dahmer and LaFleche and Segunda, and he knew immediately that whatever happened next, it would happen as a team.

Orion huddled up with the others, who had instinctively donned their Mani masks, and he leaned heavily on his Mani staff as LaFleche drew out a battle plan in the manner of a seasoned football quarterback. "It's third down and long, men, and there's no home field advantage in this here game." He kneeled down on one knee and slid his protector deity mask to the top of his head. "In terms of primary operations, we've used *special reconnaissance* and *direct action* with modest success. But there's no time for the former, and the latter looks like real trouble to me. Hell, we don't even know how many we're up against yet!"

"Been there, done that," affirmed Dahmer, raising his skeleton mask as he spoke.

"So what's the plan, man?" said Orion, speaking through his clueless, bright gold facemask while girding his red robe with the aforementioned hide belt. "Is there another kind of tactical operation we can try?"

"You bet your bells, golden boy," said LaFleche squinting up at Orion. "At third and long, it's time we tried what is fondly referred to as *unconventional warfare*." He looked around at the collection of masked faces surrounding him—the faces of extreme happiness and sadness of human suffering, the exaggerated faces of clowns, demons, deities, and mascot animals—and an idea must have occurred to him right then and there in the middle of the huddle. "Now, the way I see it is this … we know that the skill set of our paramilitary players is impressive, to say the least. What we need, right here, right now, is a *force-multiplier*—that is, a means by which we can focus and thereby increase our mechanism-of-action while managing to avoid collateral damage at the same time."

"That's a tall order, coach," said Dahmer. "How do you suggest we go about it?"

LaFleche responded patiently, as if a *time-out* had been called in the midst of all the fulminating chaos and confusion of the world around them. He carefully drew a "road" in the dirt with his finger, and on that dirt road he placed four rectangular boxes with wheels, representing the canvas-covered army trucks. "We can see from here that the fourth truck is nearly empty, so all we need to do is disable it."

"Roger that," said Dahmer.

"What we need to know is what's downrange in the other three," continued LaFleche, drawing a large circle around the three lead trucks that were parked with their front ends already heading toward the elevated plateau of Tibet. "And we can gain that intel by initiating a diversionary tactic … right here at the third truck," he said, drawing a smaller circle around the third box. "And we do that with the help of our theatrical support personnel." As Segunda explained the basic game plan to the team of Mani performers who had gathered around the huddle, LaFleche made his general intentions clear to his main offensive team. "Without putting any of these fine gentlemen directly in harm's way, we are about to use some theatrical stagecraft focused directly at our target audience … using high drama to flush the bad guys out."

"What, exactly, can I do to help?" asked Orion.

"You stay close by with Segunda and the ponies, and prepare to move up fast on my signal," said LaFleche, drawing a purposeful line in the sand. "You'll need to provide cover and proper weapons for each of us shooters as the plot goes downrange." With that, LaFleche rubbed out the primitive line drawing with his hand and lowered his face mask as he stood upright.

What happened next would have shivered the timbers and warmed the cockles of ol' Shakespeare himself. For never on the streets of fair Verona, where ancient grudges doeth break to new mutinies, did ever a walking shadow of a more noble a player strut and fret his fleeting hour upon such a stage as this—and this, all this, for the benefit of another, whom he would never know.

———————————

LaFleche strutted and fretted with enormous theatrical aplomb right up to the front of the third army truck, where he proceeded to rap his Mani staff on the windshield in the manner of a conductor gaining the attention of both an orchestra and a mulling audience.

"You cannot liberate me, General Mao, I can only liberate myself!" he shouted to the astonished driver, who may have been sleeping, but who was now assuredly wide awake.

"You cannot liberate me, General Mao, I can only liberate myself!" LaFleche repeated again, in English no less, as he dashed his staff against the cold steel of the protected grillwork. He was joined by the troupe of Mani dancers, who must have thought that the truck itself was inhabited by demons, judging by the manner in which they prodded and threatened the stricken vehicle with their

Mani staffs. Leaping high into the air, they issued great whoops and calls as they danced around the truck.

At first, their loud cries were diverse and discordant; issued, of course, in the vernacular of their local tongue. However, the theatrical repetition of the leading thespian's opening aphorism was repeated with such drama and emotion that all of the Mani dancers and, in fact, many of the bewildered bystanders soon began issuing, in unison, the same truncated refrain: "You cannot liberate me, General Mao!"

The diversion was more than sufficient to allow Dahmer to casually slip a knife blade into each of the front tires of the fourth truck. Meanwhile, the performance of the Mani dancers drew the attention of more and more uniformed Maoists, who may or may not have understood either the intellectual content or the original derivation of the phrase. Nonetheless, it was abundantly clear that they didn't like the outburst—not one bit. What was equally clear was the surprising lack of leadership, in that not one of the uniformed detractors appeared to have the remotest clue how to stifle this particular civil unrest.

"You can lead a Maoist to slaughter, but you can't make him think!" said LaFleche to Dahmer, who had just returned to his side. With a watchful eye on the disposition of his increasingly disgruntled audience, LaFleche masterfully choreographed the theatrical exorcism with careful attention to detail, keeping the Mani performers safely away from the immediate grasp of the Maoists. When the troops of armed Maoists had aggregated to such an extent as to be measured as a discernable mass, he signaled for Orion and Segunda to bring the line of tethered big-headed ponies up in front of the Mani dancers, forming a natural livestock barricade and a screen for the next dramatic act. The offensive drama of the scene intensified considerably when Dahmer and LaFleche pulled their M4A1 assault rifles out from the packs that were lashed to the sides of the equine ramparts and began spewing full-metal-jacketed bullets into the uniformed troops.

The ponies lurched and strained against their reins as Orion struggled to hold two of the frightened pack animals in place. The firing continued as the startled Maoists scattered and fell all around them. In a matter of thirty seconds, the target audience was largely disbursed or deceased, and the normal, healthy traders and pilgrims were heading for the hills in every direction. In the midst of all the dust and commotion, Orion could hear the distinctive screams of women and children coming from the foremost army trucks up the road. He ran fast to catch up with Segunda, who was already moving toward the lead trucks, but before they could even reach the spot, some thirty yards away, both the first and second truck started moving away in great haste, picking up speed as the screams of the women and children faded away in a thick cloud of dust. Looking back with an expression of sheer desperation, Orion saw Dahmer hanging out the side window of truck number three as it veered wildly onto the road, alternately firing at what was left of the uniformed targets and waving frantically for Orion and Segunda to join them on the run.

Orion and Segunda piled over the tailgate of the truck with abandon, landing at the feet of some authentic Mani dancers, who had obviously thought it would be a good idea to exit this theater of operation with the leading players. Their harsh landing in the back of the army truck was cushioned by the baskets and expedition packs that the Mani performers had surprisingly managed to load into the vehicle. These Mani dancers may not have been trained in the nuances of paramilitary special operations, nor drilled in the rifle-to-pistol transitions befitting a downrange gunfighter, but when it came to exorcising political demons, they sure knew how to keep their heads in the game; and when the game plan switched from running and gunning to the desperate business of SERE (survival, evasion, resistance, and escape), their impromptu performance on the dusty center of the street at high noon would have passed muster in any after-action critique.

The bed of the truck bucked fiercely as they picked up speed, and the Mani dancers, along with Segunda and Orion, were forced to hold on tightly to the interior supports to avoid being thrown into the air. As the rapidly accelerating vehicle careened along the unpaved road at breakneck speed, Orion made his way hand over hand to the front of the cargo bay, where he used his explorer knife to cut away the canvas covering. He was greeted by the cheeky grimace of Dahmer, who pressed his face sideways up against the rear window of the cab like a bratty child on a routine family vacation. Beside Dahmer, in the driver's seat, LaFleche was frantically double clutching, attempting to shift the transmission into a higher gear before hammering the pedal to the metal.

Orion motioned with his hand for Dahmer to move out of the way, and then Orion kicked hard. A corner of the cab window shattered into shards; shards which Dahmer proceeded to clear out entirely with the stock of his M4 rifle. "Nice of you to join us, Orion!" he shouted. "You sure know how to make an entrance—but you could have asked us *nicely* to stop for ya!" His grimacing burlesque of a smile was far more expressive than a ludicrous parody of emotion simply meant to entertain; it was more akin to the dire necessity of gallows humor, wherein the consolation of the comical is simply the flipside of the tragedy inherent in the drama of every life-and-death struggle. In any event, it was clear enough for Orion to see that Dahmer was totally in his element.

They raced out into the expanse of a wide-open landscape surrounded by multicolored mountains on all sides. Heading to the left of the snowy peaks of the Gurla Mandhata, the road followed the flow of the Karnali upstream for what seemed to Orion like hours. They wound their way over the great treeless plateau, slowly gaining ground on the pair of fleeing trucks that now appeared before them as two small dust clouds rising up from the abject desolation of the sun-scorched landscape. They gained more ground when the road turned away from the river and began to climb steadily uphill, coursing gradually around the western flanks of the great snow-capped massif.

When they finally closed within firing range of the nearest truck, Dahmer leaned far out the window and, without wasting ammunition or endangering the lives of what was considered to be the most vital cargo, he proceeded to take out two of the right rear tires. The truck wobbled to the side and veered off the road like a wounded animal before grinding its way to a halt. Before the captors could even think about harming the passengers, LaFleche pulled their truck alongside within inches of the driver's window, and Dahmer promptly blasted the cab and its contents. It was Segunda who moved next. Bounding out over the tailgate of the one truck in a flash and into the rear of the other, he proceeded to empty the contents of the cargo bay of two very dead soldiers, whose camouflage uniforms had not done them the least bit of good among the modest attire of the villagers, porters, and schoolchildren who soon exited the cargo bay more gracefully, without so much of a scratch.

Orion watched carefully, expectantly as the villagers and porters and rescued schoolchildren were carefully unloaded, but there was not a single recognizable face in the crowd, and there were no Peace Corps volunteers to be found among them.

LaFleche walked up and placed his hand on Segunda's shoulder as he nodded and smiled with approval. "I think it would be best for all concerned if we lighten our load and send the Mani dancers back with these villagers to their homes." Segunda nodded and began to translate these intentions to the Mani dancers, all of whom seemed to appreciate the wisdom of such excellent discretion as being the better part of valor. Turning back to face Dahmer and to elbow Orion— who was squinting at the receding dust cloud with an expression of affliction bordering on agony—LaFleche made another profound announcement: "The sooner you guys can unhook some spare tires, the sooner these good guys can escape back to the Limi Valley, and the sooner we can get on with our program of chasing the bad guys!"

Leaving the rescued porters and hostages in the capable hands of the Mani performers, the clandestine strike team was off again in hot pursuit. However, the distances were now of such magnitude, and the natural dereliction of the landscape in the far western corner of the Tibetan Plateau was of such colossal grandeur, as to make this headlong chase scene appear as though it were being conducted in slow motion. Seconds and minutes and miles per hour soon became all but meaningless to Orion, as time itself wound out and stretched and spun like wool into a majestic tapestry of those breathless moments of freedom from both regret and anticipation of tomorrow that rob the living of the eternal present only to melt back into the parched and barren sands of the endless desert of the worried mind. LaFleche drove on at full throttle with Dahmer at his side preparing his weapons, Segunda observing their progress through the smashed-out rear window of the cab, and Orion searching the expedition packs for field glasses that would provide them with a better view.

With the lightened load, LaFleche began to gain on the remaining truck, which appeared to be moving more slowly now as the road began to rise in altitude at the approach to the Gurla La pass. The distance between the two vehicles closed ever so slowly as they moved up the increasing incline. LaFleche was forced to shift into lower and lower gears to maintain forward progress, which slowed the chase to a crawl.

"There's no way I can catch up with them before they clear the pass!" shouted LaFleche with a note of desperation.

"Yeah, I can see that," replied Dahmer. "But now they know we are faster than they are—unless they lighten their load!"

"I was thinking the same thing!" shouted LaFleche as he down-shifted the transmission yet again.

Orion steadied himself and leaned forward into the cab, attempting to focus the field glasses on the dust cloud beyond the windshield. "I can't make out anything behind the canvas curtains!" he said, and then he handed the field glasses to Dahmer.

Finally, they crested the pass and, as the truck heaved forward and began to gain speed, they were stunned by the appearance of two gigantic lakes lying side by side in a broad basin of ruddy iron and sulfurous yellow ground. The lake on the left was narrowed and constricted into the crescent shape of a waning moon, while the lake on the right was more spherical and uniform in diameter, creating a mental juxtaposition of the crescent moon with the image of an aquatic sun. The lakes were separated physically by a narrow isthmus; it was on this narrow isthmus that the road ahead of them traced its path after a long downhill run.

"It looks like they gained about a mile and a half on us!" exclaimed Dahmer.

"I can tell that much without the glasses," replied LaFleche, vehemently shifting through the gears with the truck now barreling down the hill.

"It looks like they're moving slower at the approach to that land bridge. No, wait! It looks to me like they're stopping!"

"I don't have a good feeling about this!" shouted LaFleche, his burly knuckles clamped to whiteness on the wheel.

"They're stopped for sure!" said Dahmer. "What the hell? There's some kind of ruckus at the back of the truck ... I can see uniforms and women and children—"

"Go on! Go on!" encouraged Orion. "Tell me what you see!"

"I can see that they're running—oh God, they're running into the water! Wait! It looks like feathers coming out of nowhere! I can see dust—dust and feathers blowing across the water! It looks like we have a whole flock of young ladies on the lake!"

11. Blessings from Above

---

*A*h, *lives of men!* remarked Aeschylus, the soldier and playwright of ancient Greece who penned the tomes of *Prometheus Bound* and other notable tragedies. *When prosperous they glitter—like a fair picture; when misfortune comes—a wet sponge at one blow has blurred the painting.* It was directly into this blurred painting where misfortune had come and gone in a cloud of dust and feathers that Orion and the strident action heroes of the long range reconnaissance patrol were thrust, diving into what brave futility remained to be found floating upon the waters, opposing by all means what measures of outrageous fortune could be remedied by bringing in the dying and resuscitating the dead.

Into the poisonous, sulfurous waters of Rakas Tal (demon lake) bounded Orion with no thought in his mind but to reach for those receding Pleiades of youth and beauty that lingered but a moment or two above the surface before sinking into that bitterness of oblivion from which there could be no remission. He was soon joined by Dahmer and LaFleche, who had managed to remove their heavy boots and strip to the waist before plunging headlong into the provisional rescue mission. One by one, they dragged the limp, the lifeless, and the still-shivering bodies of women and children from the gripping glacial cold of this toxiferous lake and onto the stark, pebbled terraces of the windswept beaches, where Segunda—who apparently had never learned to swim—cut loose their bindings about the wrists and attended to their breathing and also to their bleeding, whatever the case might be.

It was with one decisive blow that the wet sponge of grave misfortune had come—by means of a fatal bullet—to Orion's beloved Joycelyn that day, forever blurring the fair and unblemished image of his long-lost Überjoy, who now lay silent and still among the bodies of the other Peace Corps volunteer teachers. Somehow, the women had managed by clever distraction to shield a significant number of the beleaguered schoolchildren from the onslaught of the executioners' bullets. It was clear from the bullet-shredded sleeping bags, which were still bleeding down and feathers into the water and the wind, that the teachers had all died waving their bedrolls; bedrolls unfurled like banners; banners streaming on the chivalric lances of courageous knights-errant. Thus, their virtuous self-sacrifice had served to deliver a final tutorial worth recording: that each and every life well-spent can be of considerable value and benefit to the next.

Orion stood there shivering in the shallows with his fists clenched tightly in anger and anguish. He surveyed the lake for more survivors and, finding none, he joined the others on a raised terrace, attending to those precious few who still needed attending, warming those who still had a need for blankets, fighting bravely against those cold fingers of death and despair that reached menacingly into the sinews of the living.

"I can't tell you how sorry I am for your loss, Orion," said LaFleche. "There are no words to describe how bad I feel for you—for all of us," he added.

"She sure is one beautiful woman," said Dahmer, looking down at Joycelyn and the others lying dead in the gravel and sand. "In fact, they all are … still beautiful in every way. Let them stay as they lay in peace, dude. We've still got a job to do."

"I know you must think that your world has come to an end, and that you've got no more reason to carry on," said LaFleche to Orion with genuine sincerity. "But I want you to know that you are more than welcome to join us. As far as I'm concerned, you've earned that right. I know that there is some part of you that is just the same as

Dahmer and me. Guys like us can't stop the gnawing urge to purge the world of all the bad guys. Guys like us will be kicking down doors and rescuing damsels in distress until the end of time."

"There is a part of me that desperately wants to go with you," said Orion. "There's no denying that."

"Then let's get a move on, bro," said Dahmer. "Those murderers are sure as shootin' laying down more miles between us and them as we speak."

"As much as I appreciate what you guys tried to do—what you did for me—and all that you mean to me—I just can't go with you any further." Orion looked over at the dead body of Joycelyn Eberhard. Then, struggling to maintain a brave face against the persistent flow of tears, he continued. "Everything that I came for is already lying here at my feet."

"She's dead, dude," implored Dahmer. "Come away with us tonight."

"What about you, Segunda?" asked LaFleche. "Can't you talk some second-hand sense into him like you did before?"

Segunda rose up from the ground, where he was attending to the minor wounds of a surviving Nepalese Sherpa child. "It is with a voluntary start that a man takes hold of his own consciousness, though he finds himself to be but half awake. He starts by running a doubtful parallel between the road ahead and all the hours that have just elapsed; he manages to emerge from one mystery by passing through a fire which he cannot control and is borne onward into yet another mystery that plunges him farther into the wilderness of a shadowy world that simply exists, without wonder or dismay. In such a shadowy world as this, a man might need a competent guide to find his way home."

"I reckon that means you're staying here with Orion," said LaFleche. "That's good, I guess," he added. And then, after he and Dahmer had sorted out the gear and mounted into the army truck, LaFleche called out through the open driver's window, "I want you both to know that you are always welcome at my campfire!" And then the truck roared off with a vengeance, shifting into higher and higher gears as the sound and the fury of the over-revved engine disappeared into the distance beyond the gloaming span of dusk.

With the onset of more deaths and darkness, Orion could not hold out any longer. Feeling neither hunger, nor cold, nor pain, he curled up alongside the stiffening body of his beloved Überjoy, though her skin was already purple and waxy and the delicate lids covering her eyes were already sinking deeper into the recesses of her skull. He held onto her body tightly with the intention that he would sooner have his own bones crumble to dust than allow himself to be separated ever again from the one he loved so dearly. With the passage of the evening hours, Segunda's compassion must have been piqued to the point of a gentle intervention, of sorts.

"O Heroic One, what must a good man do when remorse itself assumes the shape and features of his mortally wounded lover? How should a good man behave when that fiend of dread comes draped in her womanly garments, with a pale beauty upon the face that still lingers amid this desolation, and lies down by his side?"

Orion slowly released his grip from around Joycelyn's lifeless body, and he drew himself up to his knees beside her. "You're right, Segunda. I feel within myself the likeness of a corpse, shrouding me with some dark and bloody stain upon my very soul. I feel my heart withering and sinking into a wintry gloom. I know it is not her spirit but some unknown hand that compels me to move deeper and deeper into this nightmare realm that blends itself with the darkness of the crypt."

Segunda bent down on one knee, and he whispered such that only Orion, and no one else, could hear. "It is by desperate effort that you start upright, breaking the bonds of that fiendish, semiconscious sleep. It is by desperate effort and eternal overcoming that you take up arms against these feelings of darkness and despair. You must strive above all strivings to realize that these specters of dire delusion exist solely in your *haunted mind*. Your eyes of flesh must search for something, anything that might remind you of the living world around you."

"Yes, yes, Segunda. I am searching for something." Orion's

eyes gazed wildly around the night scene, catching only glimpses of the faint votive lights emitted through the small, dingy windows of the nearby gompas and the blurred luster of the dying campfires commending their last watery reflections upon the lakes. He closed his eyes again and lowered his head to her body as he spoke. "I am searching for a place and time before this darkness swallowed the whole of my happiness." His body drooped, and his head fell back upon the pillow of her chest. "How pleasant it would be to dream this beauty back again," he muttered. "How nice to feel the rise and fall of a tender bosom, a softer breathing than my own. How glad I am to feel the quiet throb of a purer heart imparting its peacefulness unto my troubled mind. How pleasant my solitude would be."

Segunda left Orion there where he lay, knowing that he had intentionally moved beyond all reason, as though the hysterical fondness of the troubled dreamer was actively summoning all those that were dearly departed into the gossamer fabric of his dream. Orion was allowing her influence to spread over him as they lay together beneath the stars, although she had no existence but the memories and images to which he willingly surrendered. Together, they sank down into the buoyancy of a soft, superfluous plot of land that exists on the borders of sleep and wakefulness; a place where thoughts rise up before the dreamer in cinematic pictures, sometimes unfocussed and disconnected, yet eagerly assimilated and displayed by a pervading lamplight of gladness and beauty.

Wheeling beneath the gorgeous radiance of a thousand floodlights, yet sheltered by the softening shadows of ancient banyan trees, the roadway paved with tiles of memories and pictures leads Orion down a rustic lane through the blissful mist of a summer shower, past the bright merriment of children at the gates of a schoolhouse playground and into the shades of an autumnal wood, where the twittering flights of songbirds arc across the vibrant canopy, heralding the joyful procession of a bevy of rosy girls that leads to the altar of a young man and his recent bride who entwine their bodies in the fullness of grace and dance on the floor of a splendid ballroom that sweeps across the vastness of the spot-lighted stage of a crowded theater and into that pleasant solitude of hushed romantic intimacy where two warm bodies merge to oneness as the velvet curtain of the night falls over the scene.

With morning came the help of pilgrims who were on their way north to circle Mount Kailash in a holy ritual, only to be sidetracked by the pressing need to care for the bodies of the women and the children that were worsening in the sun. Orion and Segunda assisted in the proceedings by carrying the dead bodies from the shores of the brackish demon lake across the narrow strip of land to the sweeter banks of Lake Manasarovar, whose rippled terraces led out in rings to a great expanse of glistening waters; waters as clear as could be found around its shores, yet which changed dramatically in coloration with depth and with the movements of the clouds from a gemlike cobalt blue to a deep emerald green. Owing its name, Manasarovar (lake of the mind), to the mind of the creator, Brahma, it is thought by some that to but bathe in these crystalline waters is sufficient to wash away the sins of a lifetime. As such, each of the corpses were bathed and ritualistically purified before being trussed up in makeshift sackcloth and seated, as gods that sit on lotus thrones, at the foreground of a simple whitewashed gompa that stood higher up on the bank overlooking the spectral lake.

The kindly pilgrims sent a pair of Toyota Land Cruisers back to the border town of Taklakot for firewood and medical supplies. Attention was then directed by local monks to the souls of the deceased. The recitation of sacred texts and verses were aimed at placing the newly departed face-to-face with the true nature of reality in the intermediate state, with the intention of enabling emancipation of consciousness and deliverance by hearing such helpful instructions. However, in thoughtful consideration of the distinct likelihood that not every soul in the after-death plane is capable of achieving maximal emancipation and deliverance in such an instant, the readings continued to descend in content to somewhat lower realms of rebirth, with more practical instructions on how to cope with the lesser aspects of diminishing returns. Orion reeled at the strangeness of the thoughts, and he refused to allow such funereal readings to be made over Joycelyn's dead body.

Later in the day, the Toyota Land Cruisers returned with the medical supplies and firewood, and the lifeless bodies of all but Überjoy were moved higher up onto a level embankment to be cremated. Carried in a litter chair one by one like high personages, the deceased were seated—with figurative lotus flowers and kindling beneath them—as the funeral pyres were erected like miniature temples around each woman and child. With the setting of the sun, the pyres were finally lit on fire and the bodies were seen in sharp decline, sent up in a huge conflagration of smoke and flames.

When darkness fell, Orion made his way to the same spot, wishing to return with her to that soft, superfluous plot of land that exists on the border of sleep and wakefulness and dreams of eternal beauty. Again, Orion refused to be swayed or comforted by the imploring words of Segunda. Again, he held onto her body tightly with the same resolve that he would sooner have his own bones crumble to dust than allow himself to be separated from his beloved Überjoy. Orion spoke not a single word as he lay there by her side, waiting devoutly to die in her arms, aching to sleep that eternal sleep with her and her alone.

The next morning, Segunda became somewhat impatient with the mournful progress of his charge. And so he endeavored, quite decisively, to rouse the heartsick lover with a challenging diatribe designed to awaken the would-be-dead.

"Oh, what a quaint and precious world you Westerners dreamed up to help you sleep at night! What a fairytale existence you believe in—when everything happens *Once Upon a Time*! It was *once upon a time* when the sons of god walked upon the earth. *Once upon a time*, the mighty prophets spoke with an eloquence of the angels. *Once upon a time*, the ancients built great tombs and temples with ideals that would civilize the planet. *Once upon a time*, you dreamed you had found a love and a relationship that would last forever. How quaint! How precious! How wrong! Everything that existed *then* exists *now*, as it shall again. Even your esteemed Darwin knew that the origins of life itself would be born anew if it were not cannibalized and predated by existing forms and beings that are aggressively competing for and co-opting the same biological niche."

Orion was unmoved by the chastising appeals of Segunda, and he held onto the body of his beloved Überjoy with all the fury of his soul. In fact, Orion would surely have given his blood, his entrails, his fame, his salvation, and his own life in this world and the next just to see a trace of her slightest smile, to feel the warmth of her living body, to caress her feet, her arms, her shoulders, her splendid breasts, to sense the pulse of her heart and its vital flow through the contours of her delicate blue veins, to savor the fragrance of her vibrant skin, and to relish in the solace of her embrace, one more time.

"While you are bemoaning the loss of what you once experienced with Joycelyn Eberhard, *once upon a time,* you should realize that she needs you *now* more than ever! It is *now,* at the time of her departure, that she truly needs your greatest devotion!"

Orion looked up at Segunda with curiosity, for he could scarcely recall a single occasion—save for Segunda's attack in defense of the Mani dancers—in which he had appeared so vocally incensed.

"It is not enough for you, O Heroic One, to exhaust yourself in the process of bringing in the injured and the dying; it is time for you to rise to the necessity of this very moment—it is time for you to attend to the conveyance of the dead! Of all the things you ever carried over distances far and wide, this is perhaps your most important burden—it is the labor of your love."

Segunda paused in his dictation as Orion loosened his embrace of Joycelyn's dead body and looked up to him with an extremely perplexed expression, squinting into the hazy brightness of the early morning sun. And then Segunda continued: "If and when you manage to rise to this momentous occasion, it could be your finest hour!"

Disregarding Segunda's impassioned speech, Orion lay motionless in the dust for quite some time; that is, until he felt a soft and warm and gentle hand upon his back … and then another. It was the surviving schoolchildren, who were preparing to leave with a group of the returning pilgrims, all of whom had altered their scheduled pilgrimage to help these children find their way to some form of sanctuary. Each of the surviving schoolchildren was silently paying their final respects to Joycelyn and to Orion with the passing touch of their hands. Orion looked up, and this time he was amazed to see a sparkling likeness of Joycelyn Eberhard in the reflections of a child's eyes. It was in this child's eyes that he saw the doorway to eternity. It was in the sweet and unassuming innocence of these eyes that Orion caught the merest glimpse of the sparkling resolve and idealism that reminded him so much of Joycelyn's original purpose. And then they were gone.

In the interval that followed, Orion realized something that had hitherto eluded him entirely: *Neither of them, as individuals, could have managed to save these little ones alone. It required both of them working in unison: she, with her heartfelt dedication to teaching, service, and self-sacrifice, had provided much-needed education in language and values and culture; he, with his unshakeable resolve to hunt and chase with a keen aim toward rescue, had marshaled the necessary resources and wherewithal to accomplish the nearly impossible—together, they managed the survival of these few innocents and an increase in their quality of life. Together, these star-crossed Americans and their colleagues had set an example that raised the bar in the field of human caring for one another in extremis. And it was this example of caring that now shone in the eyes of these war-torn survivors.*

Orion finally kissed his beloved one last time and drew himself up to his full stature. "Okay, Segunda, I may be dense, but I'm not dead yet. You were saying something about conveyance ...."

Standing Orion's expedition pack upright on its supportive internal frame, Segunda emptied it of all military hardware and unnecessary contents and, with the help of two kindly monks, he sat the once rigor-hardened but now noticeably limp body of Joycelyn Eberhard on the ground with her back up against the nylon fabric, folding her still-lovely legs up with her knees to her chin, and lashing her compacted body directly to the compressed pack. Using the rainfly of Orion's wishful two-man tent, Segunda trussed her death-tinged body even more securely for its final journey, while Orion looked on with an expression of disbelief bordering on anaphylactic shock. Orion turned away and stood stoically upright while the monks lifted the package and Segunda helped it onto Orion's broad shoulders.

In silence, Orion followed Segunda and the monks up the gravel road that led between the two disparate lakes and onward to the north, where a footpath diverged from the main jeep road that curved off to the right toward Lhasa, some two thousand kilometers to the east. They were joined by two additional Tibetan monks with broad brimmed hats, saffron yellow wraps, and robes the color of dove's blood. The monks carried their own small backpacks comprised of little more than burlap sacks bound with hemp rope, and they walked with the aid of staffs, not unlike those of the Mani dancers of Nepal. Orion, on the other hand, carried nothing in his hands nor in his thoughts, which were now as empty as the sky itself, intensely blue with extreme clarity, yet devoid of a single vestige of a tear.

The trek to the north was long and hard; all the while, the towering flanks of a gigantic black rock, cut by some unseen hand into the exquisite shape of a diamond, loomed up before them. It was Mount Kailash—that most venerated of all Himalayan mountains and, at the same time, the least-visited holy place—that mythical Axis Mundi (center of the world) of the Eastern world where the earth and the sky and all four directions of the compass meet in a tangible point of beginning, dissemination, and departure—that favorite abode of the Hindu god, Shiva, destroyer of ignorance and delusion, who lives atop the mountain practicing yogic austerities while, at the same time, making joyous love in tantric union with his divine consort— that soaring contradiction of awe and wonder that stands head and shoulders above all its surroundings, that colossal jewel that defies all geological comparisons, that massive snowcapped shrine that simply shines as it exists with the power of its own nature.

They stopped for the night at Tarboche, a barren, windswept place where a giant pole with great ropes of prayer flags is bedecked anew each spring in a sacred Buddhist festival. The flagpole is repositioned in a massive technical pole-raising effort and held in place in such a manner that is considered to be auspicious; that is, perfectly upright and straight—in order to preclude any bad omens that might come with the slightest degree of incorrect leanings. Unfortunately, there was something that was apparently lost in translation between the attempted destruction of the Tibetan culture and religion with the onset of rabid Maoism in the 1950s and '60s and the humanistic restoration of these idiosyncratic traditions with a new generation of practitioners in more recent years, for it was apparent that the *straightness* of the current flagpole left something to be desired. It was almost as if the property of standing upright and straight had become a lost art in the modern communist state.

Orion, of course, was much too exhausted by his labors to be concerned with such historical deliberations, and after gratefully accepting a little food and water from his companions, he leaned over on his side and immediately fell asleep with the dead body of Joycelyn Eberhard still physically strapped to his back.

Orion was awakened before daybreak by the familiar voice of Segunda.

"Your breath is still ... your body is cold ... you cannot stay any longer."

It took Orion a moment to realize that Segunda was not speaking to him, but to Joycelyn.

"You cannot stay any more than a baby can stay forever in the womb."

Chills ran up and down Orion's reclining spine as he realized what was happening.

"Leave behind all you know ... all you love ...."

The mere hearing of these words was crushing, but Orion remained quiet, listening.

"Leave behind all pain and suffering," continued Segunda. "This is what death is."

Orion's heart was racing now with a new, unwelcome fear of estrangement.

"Don't be afraid," continued Segunda. "Everyone before you has died."

Segunda helped Orion to his feet by supporting the full weight of the pack. And then they were off again, climbing upward with the modest entourage of rustic holy men into a valley of slowly rising mists, where the frost on the western slopes glimmered like golden jewels in the softened glow of a reluctant morning sun. Climbing higher in altitude, they passed rows of irregularly shaped Buddhist prayer stones with arcane verses carved onto the broad slate surfaces. Some of the prayer stones were tilted upright, forming a long jagged row that lined the footpath, while many others lay side by side, facing skyward, creating acres upon acres of readings for a celestial *tableau vivant*.

They continued to climb through an eerie atmosphere of cloud-like vapors to the gentle slopes of a grassy promontory, where a group of men wearing stocking caps and filthy aprons were gathered near a small block building, standing at a vantage point that overlooked the valley floor. The heady aroma of juniper smoke filled the air with an apprehension that something both solemn and significant was about to happen. The attendants at the celestial burial site calmly approached Orion and removed the funereal pack from his back and placed it gently upon four crude rocks that kept the frame off the ground. Segunda ushered Orion away from the spot as the monks began to chant with the accompaniment of chimes and the attendants unbound the body for the next stage of the funeral.

The juniper incense apparently served a purpose to summon the assistance of nature to the ceremony, for an increasing number of impressively large vultures appeared in the steamy haze overhead, and they began to land and to gather in an ominous crowd on the upper slopes of the hillside, appearing as a dull gray congregation of mourners that were waiting for the service to begin.

"You should imagine that those are *dakinis*, the Tibetan equivalent of angels," said Segunda to Orion, who was obviously becoming increasingly uncomfortable with the proceedings. "In Tibetan, the word 'dakini' means *sky dancer*," continued Segunda. "As the monks call the consciousness from the body, the dakinis will take the consciousness from the body to the heavens, which is understood to be a windy place where thoughts, emotions, and memories dissolve, and the soul awaits its emancipation or reincarnation into the next life."

"I don't mind if they watch," said Orion. "I just don't want those vultures getting any part of her."

"You must become stronger than that, O Heroic One," said Segunda. "If she is truly fortunate and the *rogyapas*, the body breakers, do their job well, the dakinis will assuredly take all of her!"

Orion trembled with the force of the shuddering revelation, and he steeled himself with all his might, knowing full well that he had run completely out of alternatives.

When the monks finished chanting, the attendants lifted Joycelyn's body onto a large rectangular stone slab that looked like an altar, of sorts. However, when they tied a rope around her neck and affixed the other end of the rope to a stake in the ground, the function of the cold stone slab as a butcher's bench became stunningly clear. With purposeful, skillful strokes of a large carving knife, huge gaping slices were made in her back and along the lengths of her legs and arms. Orion turned away as they cut into Joycelyn's chest and abdomen to retrieve the leaden bullets that had killed her, and he flinched repeatedly with the crushing sound of heavy mallets that were applied to her bones, as if his own bones were being broken upon the altar for the blackest sins of the world.

Suddenly, some unheard signal was given, and the grim congregation of vultures began to bash their way in amongst the rogyapas, who backed away, as a rising flood of outstretched wings and monstrous feathered things converged upon the scene. More and more cinereous vultures crowded in as their powerful beaks and menacing skull-like heads disappeared into a grizzly molten tapestry of grey-brown feathers, forming a blessed cloak of a funeral shroud that hid the naked singularity of human carnage from the directness of vulgar view. For more than thirty minutes—what seemed like a lifetime—chittering waves of vultures joined the feeding frenzy, until such point in time that the tempestuous devouring of the greedy birds was halted by the rogyapas, who scattered and shooed the vultures away with loud shouts and waving sticks, revealing the horrific remains of a bloody skeleton still tied to the stake by the neck.

It was clearly an act of compassion that prompted Segunda to shield Orion's eyes from the vividness of such dreadful memories, as the last remnants of the cranium and spinal column were shattered to splinters and pulverized to a pulp that was mixed with tsampa flour and butter and fashioned into a final mound; a mound that was eagerly distributed by the return of the cinereous vultures, followed by lesser hawks and crows, until nothing of Joycelyn remained.

There was a great flapping sound made by scores of wings surging overhead, which drew the attention of all to the dramatic departure of the enormous birds as they ascended into the clearing sky. Indeed, the feathered dakinis now appeared like angels incarnate, like graceful dancers rising up from the earthbound brume of sorrow and into that celestial theater above the world, carrying away all cruel remnants of her lifeless body as they soared away over the mountains, escorting the luminous manifestation of her soul into the highest and brightest of heavens.

Segunda himself must have been inspired by the ethereal majesty of the Tibetan sky burial, for he added an unexpected encore to the occasion. As serenity returned to the grassy promontory, and Orion drifted off into the oblivion of thoughtless quiescence, Segunda calmly reached into his pack and retrieved the blood-soaked scrolls of his vast collection of mummified ears. Although there were only a few vultures left in the foreground, there were sufficient hawks and crows remaining to make quick work of the dead Maoist scrolls, once they were properly positioned and unfurled.

12. Exodos

And then the world again grew silent as a stone. The fathomless sky, devoid of any living thing, was neither light nor dark. That once-heroic hunter who strived to seek, to save, and not to yield, was bowed by the weight of all the disheartening twilight hours that worked their will and left him nothing but burning tears of a grim despair that rises from the heart and gathers behind the eyes, beclouding his vision with a veil of sorrow, bedimming his memories of joyful days until there remained no more than dull gray shadows growing fainter with the ominous impression of emptiness that prevails when all, including love, is lost.

With the approach of sundown, Orion found himself running down the matted hillside to catch up with Segunda—for each and every man (and woman) inhabits a private world of tender thoughts and experiences which creates, at times, a sense of intense vulnerability that becomes so unbearably acute as to drive the unfortunate individual toward a preemptive consultation with someone perceived to embody the wisdom of the ages; that is, someone who seems to reflect a calm, abiding certainty that is entirely lacking in their own private world. It was as if Orion, the heartsick hunter, was reaching out for something, anything at all, any single, solitary scrap of something solid and real that might yet exist beyond his own impending emptiness when he bounded up to Segunda and burst out with a series of nearly incoherent questionings.

"There is so much emptiness, Segunda ... so much nothingness ... so much stillness all around me. What can a man hold on to ... what can a man believe ... when all that is left is but sorrow ... and aloneness ... and suffering ... and more emptiness?"

Segunda stopped in his tracks as the last rays of direct sunlight disappeared behind the distant ridges, and he slowly turned to face Orion, removing his polychromatic glacier glasses in the process.

"Tell me, Segunda! For pity sake, tell me!" pleaded Orion. "What *now* must I do?"

Segunda smiled sympathetically and nodded his head as he spoke. "You, with your own heart and mind, must seek to find what is most important to you, O Heroic One, and then you will know what needs to be done: what dreadful wrongs need to be righted; what friend in distress might benefit from your moral support; what perfect stranger is in desperate need of rescue. I cannot tell you what new chapters need to be written, what manner of potent elixir needs to be invented, what high art of aspiration needs your heroic ambition to propel you, and all humanity with you, on to the next stage of a greater glory."

"Oh! Segunda, I hear your words, but I cannot abide the incessant bellowing of my own misery! I can't return home empty-handed—I know that much! These horrifying issues of sickness and corruption of society are much too daunting for one man to even consider, let alone remedy!" Orion unshouldered his depleted expedition pack and balanced his weight on its upright frame. "You have to help me understand these difficult things, as you have in the past .... Tell me what *you* think I should do!"

"Segunda has no answers of such originality for you," he said. "As you might recall, Segunda was recruited to be your guide only when your path was firmly established and your course of action was already indelibly clear."

Orion looked to be more than disappointed—considering the advanced state of his personal sufferings—and he appeared crestfallen with a majestic sadness befitting the death of all that is blissful and beautiful in the world.

Segunda was moved to add an addendum. "However, you should

know this: When you set out to right some wrong that needs to be righted, but has not been righted yet ... when you endeavor to overcome some evil that by all standards of human decency needs to be defeated, but has not been defeated yet ... when you set about the task of fashioning some marvelous elixir for the body or the mind that should by all measures of human value be celebrated from a place beyond the highest rooftops, and yet the voices of all the earthly authorities remain only silent or shrill ... you may again find someone like Segunda, to second your own emotions and to guide you on your way."

Orion rose up to his full stature again and shouldered his pack. "I assume that you are going to be heading eastward now to look for Dahmer and LaFleche."

"Yes indeed," said the benevolent Gurkha. "From this point on, they need the assistance of Segunda more than you do."

The men shook hands in parting, and then Segunda turned and began to walk down into the valley from which they had come, moving competently with due diligence along on the ever-darkening trail. Segunda turned around one more time and, as Orion held up his outstretched arm in a final gesture of farewell, shouted out one last refrain.

"Always remember—when you set out again on that brave path that is for you and you alone to travel, you will find that the world around you is a shooting gallery—it is a consequence of your own enlightened intentions that you become the stand-up guy!"

Orion stood there alone on that lonely hillside of the Tibetan plateau for a long time while the big orange ball dropped even more conclusively over the western horizon, turning the shadowy hillsides around him into a rolling sea of delicately flushed mounds, darkening the few traipsing clouds into a myriad of deepening purples and somber grays, leaving only the gem-like facets of Mount Kailash with its conical snow-covered summit illuminated brightly in the fullness of the sunset. And then, that too grew dark.

Orion lay down upon the hillside, unbuckled the waist belt of his expedition pack, and slid his arms out from the shoulder straps. He stared up into the cold, prosaic sky with lackluster eyes, his mind filled with nothing but the dimness of remorse and an ever-darkening tincture of regret. He did not feel the movements of the restless winds that pressed down upon the mountains; he did not feel the hours in the stillness of his mind. It was only the memories of nearly forgotten moments he noticed, moments no one else could know. He stared up into that boundless maw of darkness, that unrelenting vault of expanding emptiness above, attempting to bridge the insurmountable distances between him and her and those nearly forgotten moments that now appeared like distant stars.

Even in darkness, light dawns for the upright. The next morning, Orion was terribly hungry, and yet he felt somewhat refreshed, having found a few traces of gentle radiance within the otherwise unbearable emptiness. Before him lay so many choices, so many possibilities to consider: *Should he race off to the east to join Segunda, Dahmer, and LaFleche in their mission; should he continue to circumambulate the holy Mount Kailash in a pilgrim's kora (sacred circuit) to advance his spiritual standing; should he travel back to the USA and become an emersion journalist in an effort to broadcast the sad story of human trafficking to the world; should he become a schoolteacher or fundraise for an orphanage; should he join the Peace Corps, study astronomy, write a book, or blog to the high heavens on the World Wide Web?* All of the above seemed to Orion to be equally compelling, equally feasible, equally doable, and yet, equally reprehensible in terms of his own heart's desire. There was simply no sustainable joy to be found in any of these ultimately banal and pedestrian activities. Orion strived to recall the final words of Segunda about setting out to achieve something that has never been done before—along with Segunda's fatalistic warning for any would-be stand-up person—and he felt a pleasant elevation accompanied by a curious renewal of his spirit.

The more he thought about the infinite possibilities of his own enlightened intentions, the less *attached* he felt to his own sorrow.

It was almost as though the process of attachment itself had created a form of imprisonment, as though his overwhelming desire to have and to hold—even sorrow—so firmly in his possession had created this prison, which seemed initially like hearth and home, but in reality was still a prison. Orion continued on his way with a new lightness in his step, pursuing the thought to a distant point where even the attachment to his own corporeal body was set aside, and he began to feel a new presence of mind that was comforting and familiar and assuring. Here on the windswept barrens of the Tibetan steppes, amidst the parched and desiccated highland desert that surrounded him, Orion was experiencing an oceanic feeling that comes with the realization that neither she nor he can be tethered any longer, neither to the stake nor the ground. A consciousness of all that is and all that can be arises in his thoughts; and his thoughts are invariably of her, and *with* her, and it is in this reflective awakening of his mind that he begins to discern her overarching presence.

Now, Orion knew that his relatively unsophisticated mind was no more developed than that of the next guy's, and he is certainly not to be considered adept in the meditations and ramifications of contemplative religious practice. What appeared to be happening to the erstwhile hunter is not all that uncommon in the mind(s) of anyone who truly seeks with all his heart and mind on any given day or night. His concrete mind was simply beginning to experience the world as a floating abstraction that expands like the sky, enveloping all, extending itself into the realm of infinite possibilities where there is no longer separation, but unity; where star-crossed lovers are no longer entirely apart, but are drawn together by unending love; where he and she are no longer cleaved by space and time, but find themselves everywhere as one—and *one who is everywhere is joyous.*

Orion's elevated thoughts extended to Dahmer and LaFleche. He thought of Dahmer, whose creative solution to targeting the nature of the beast with the surgical precision of his M4 rifle added an entirely new appendage to the beautiful and ferocious Durga Bhagwati, who protects her children with so many weapons and preserves moral order in the universe. He thought of LaFleche, and his strident rapping on the windshield of the Chinese army truck with nothing but a Mani staff, offering up his theatrical brand of wisdom concerning the nature and responsibilities of personal liberation. Orion began to smile as he recalled these things, reflecting on the ceaseless struggle for freedom that was going on all over the world. It was a freedom that was not merely political, nor economic, nor sociological, nor even from disease, but a ceaseless struggle for a more undisputed freedom: freedom from the mundane world of ordinary experience.

Orion recognized the acres of upward-facing prayer stones that lined a stretch of the road above Tarboche, and he scanned the horizon for the two opposing lakes of the sacred and the profane which would soon come floating into view like surrealistic mirages. In his current state of mind, these jagged slates, whether propped upright or lying flat upon the dusty ground, no longer appeared any different to him than the many flag stones, cobblestones, paving stones, benchmarks, milestones, plaques, monuments, territorial markers, corner stones, columns, memorials, cairns, footstones, gravestones, monoliths, needles, obelisks, tributes, tablets, towers, steles, and shrines that are placed at intervals along well-traveled roads to bear witness to the towering ambitions of all mankind.

With every reluctant yet determined step forward upon the Tibetan plateau, Orion felt a little less connected to the brutish, stone-cold physicality of the modern world around him. He felt a little more connected to his innermost thoughts; thoughts that now, more often than not, appertained to those lingering issues of radiance and displaced beauty that shined brightly in his mind in the midst of all the inner darkness. With every reluctant yet determined step upon this vaulted rooftop of the world, in the presence of his beloved, Orion felt a little less connected to the dullness of the earth, a little more connected to the brightness of the sky.

About the Author

Konrad Ventana, literally translated as "Bold Counsel Through a Window," is an American scientist and visionary. He looks behind the scenes at the ideologies of our modern times and examines the potential for future development. He currently lives in California.